SALVATION

SALVATION

A Novel

C. WILLIAM LANGSFELD

Counterpoint
California

SALVATION

This is a work of fiction. All of the characters, organizations, and events portrayed in this novel are either products of the author's imagination or used fictitiously.

First Counterpoint edition: 2026

Library of Congress Cataloging-in-Publication Data
Names: Langsfeld, C. William author
Title: Salvation : a novel / C. William Langsfeld.
Description: First Counterpoint edition. | San Francisco : Counterpoint, 2026.
Identifiers: LCCN 2025034660 | ISBN 9781640097230 hardcover | ISBN 9781640097247 ebook
Subjects: LCGFT: Noir fiction | Western fiction
Classification: LCC PS3612.A5848 S25 2026 | DDC 813/.6—dc23/eng/20250825
LC record available at https://lccn.loc.gov/2025034660

Jacket design by Nicole Caputo and Victoria Maxfield
Jacket photograph © iStock/KenTannenbaum
Book design by Wah-Ming Chang

COUNTERPOINT
Los Angeles and San Francisco, CA
www.counterpointpress.com

Printed in the United States of America

1 3 5 7 9 10 8 6 4 2

For Birdsong

SALVATION

Prologue

In the colorless light of early morning, at the crest of a rise on a gravel road plastered in snow and ice, Tom Horak cut the motor on the brown Dodge pickup and the white smoke billowing from the rusted pipe faltered in the frigid January air.

He sat for a long time. The windows condensed with moisture, frost building in the corners.

Tom stepped down from the truck.

A red-faded-to-orange down jacket lacquered by dirt with an oily sheen, patch of duct tape on the bottom right by the sheath of the zipper. He pulled the fringes of a dark blue sock hat down where it had pushed up above his ears. Hair held together in greasy streaks lay against the skin of his neck above the shoulder. A skimpy beard, thin and even on the cheeks, denser along the chin. His leather boots squeaked in the snow and the report from the closing door was muffled by spruce in the creek bottom that ran along the road. He pulled the puffed hood of his jacket over his head and walked down the slope of the road, his breathing tight and short. A filter of high clouds obscured the sky. *Storm's coming*, he thought.

Before he saw the other truck he could hear it. The incessant chug of the motor. A slow fog of exhaust. The only car in the wide plowed-out area at the end of the road. A line of snowmobiles in varying stages of submersion were parked on the edge of the uphill side of the clearing; here and there along the snowbound road beyond the trailhead more of the machines were scattered about. Left by locals for recreation or to commute to off-grid cabins and homes in the mountains. Mounds of willows in the ravine poked up through the white like periscopes from the underbrush.

Tom knew the pickup. An off-white Chevy with a horizontal strip of red on the side panels. The truck belonged to Rust Hawkins. A man he'd known for damn near all his life, though the friendship had died ages ago. If pressed, Tom would not have been able to explain the logic of the events that led him to this time and place, and it was not love that he carried with him in his heart on that cold winter morning.

He approached the truck, its open bed half filled with snow and the lumps of objects buried there. The bench seat spanned the width of the narrow cab. A gun rack in the rear window held a Winchester Model 70 hunting rifle.

From that vantage, there did not appear to be anyone in the truck, but Tom knew better.

He walked on. The *cree-cree* of his boots in the hard snow fast-forwarded and did not slow until he'd reached the door, pulling it open without thought. Rust was inside, hunched over with his back to the open door. Tom grabbed the collar of Rust's jacket and yanked from behind so Rust fell backward, headlong onto the ice. Tom turned and fell on top of him, knees in Rust's chest and hands on his face, pressed against the familiar features. Tom's hate bubbled out through spittle and sweat and fear. Rust struggled and his head bucked. Then Tom felt a sharpness in the meat of the outside of his left palm as Rust sank a canine into the flesh there and Tom fell to the side. Clutched at his hand while his head and shoulder were buoyed by the open door. He rolled to the ground and the two men lay beside each other, shifting and aimless, Rust with a bit of blood from Tom's hand smeared in his teeth, drawing from the corner of his mouth.

Goddamnit, Tom, said the man. You cunt-lickin son of a bitch. Rust pushed then pulled himself up. You fuckin twat.

Rust rose to a kneeling position and scrambled into the cab. The Model 70 was there in the gun rack held in place by rubber-coated hooks mounted to the glass of the rear window, and he reached toward it, curses coming like garbled reflexes, indiscernible and automatic. Took hold of the barrel and slipped it from the hook behind the passenger seat as Tom grabbed him by the ankle, yanking backward. Rust gripped the hunting rifle and the earth fell from beneath him. He dropped from the front seat with a pop. The walnut butt of the Winchester pivoted, forced through the square glass window, and granules of translucent shrapnel exploded through the back of the cab, caught the light as they scattered and vanished in the snow.

Tom rolled over and scrambled onto Rust's back as his former friend tried to rise, the weight of Tom holding him, driving his elbows and forearms into his back, pressing him, one hand on the back of his head, fingers clutched at the dry sandy hair. Groping through the roots he affirmed an iron grip at the scalp level and the other hand rotated the length of rifle until the wrist that held it turned back on itself and Rust cried out. Tom pulled the rifle across the back of Rust's neck. Placed a shin over each end of the gun, pinning the man, both hands driving his face into the ice that was turning pink then red in the early light. Blood and snot and saliva splattered out the side of Rust's mouth in equine bursts of forced exhale. Then something in Rust's neck shifted beneath the walnut. Through the wood and metal Tom felt a rasping vibration like rough chunks of slate sliding over one another inside a bundle of blankets. The body spasmed. Limbs twitched with electricity and a gurgling seeped from the face that lay hidden in the frozen ground. Electric currents in Rust's nerves pulsed and then died, and the body beneath Tom went limp.

Tom slumped against the cab of the pickup. Arm rested on the floorboard and his head down, eyes closed. After a moment he reached across with his right hand and turned the key in the ignition. The motor died and a buzzing filled the air until he pulled the key out and let it fall to the floor.

Full day had risen. A grouping of chickadees *rat-a-tat-tat*-ed in some tree out of sight. Tom smelled the frozen air, the metal, the woods. Looked up at the sky. A brief piercing cold on his forehead. He blinked. It had begun to snow. Small, thin flakes hazed the view at a distance. He pulled himself to a kneeling position and let the rifle teeter to one side. His knees slipped to the ground and a dampness soaked through the fabric of his pants. The snow fell harder now. Already the dead man had a layer of white accumulating like mold.

He began to walk beyond the trailhead, away from the trucks. The road beneath feet of packed snow unfolded before him and nothing registered. Everything was white, and beyond the white, a pale nothing. He walked. *Goddamnit, Rust. You motherfucker.* Tom's body shook. He was crying now. Arms flung out at random. He stomped and jumped. *Why you got to do that? He didn't deserve that. He's just a boy. Your fuckin son.* He hit himself in the face with a full open palm. The pain was clear and crisp and made sense. The only thing that made any sense. *Goddamnit, Rust.* He was still moving up the snow-bound road, farther than cars could go. Past a few of the snowmobiles that were parked in the ditches and on the hillside until he came to a grouping of them. He investigated. Found one with a key. In a small town no one gave thought to thieves because, generally speaking, there were none. It was not a matter of trust so much as a practicality. Why protect against something that does not exist? Like churchgoers paying homage to a God that has no heed for wood or brick or nails.

Tom grabbed the pull cord and gave it a yank. It was stubborn, sticking at first, and then it pulled easy, the motor turning and not firing until it did and the machine sputtered to life with a choke and a backfire and a cloud of blue smoke. *Fuck yeah*, thought Tom. *Fuck everything.* He saddled up and throttled out. Paused and spun around. At the truck everything was as he'd left it. The cooling body wet and covered in snow. Pool of bloody slush beside the head. The rifle was there. He rummaged behind the seats and gathered up the loose cartridges he could find. Shouldered the rifle slantwise across his back and left the civilized world behind.

PART I

Marshal Tomlinson

*T*he call come in the early part of midmorning. Well, not a call, but Colton Westcliff come into the office. Come down by snowmobile from his cabin in the Elks and saw Harry Boneview, the plow driver from the county, who sent him on into town because Colton was headed that way anyhow. Didn't know about the body or didn't say nothin. I don't think he knew. Harry just told him to fetch the marshal and that's what he done.

Me and my first deputy, Lawrence White, we went on up to check it out. When we got up there they wasn't no tracks to be seen. Over a foot of snow had come down on top of it by then. Lawrence was beside himself. Asked if we shouldn't secure the perimeter. Secure it from what? I told him to knock himself out. Kind of walked a quick lap, eyes scannin the woods, and met me and Harry at a half-plowed snowbank stickin out from the scoop of his plow. Not the only thing stickin out.

The trucks were easy enough to identify, as was the body, once we got him thawed out a bit. Rust Hawkins, longtime resident of the valley. Almost said member of the community there, though that would be a stretch. Kind of a loner is how I always thought of him. Later we called into school and they said his boy wasn't in. "Unexcused absence" they called it. Course Tom Horak was involved. We figured that much since his truck was there. Can't say how exactly. Everythin's a theory for the moment, innocent until and all that, but it don't look good for him. Makes sense I guess, given their history. Then again, nothin about this situation makes any goddamn sense.

Tom

The world was white and fear and darkness. Even in the daylight, sun obscured by thick clouds and snowfall, Tom saw only darkness. The snowmobile roared through the fresh snow, piling up in inches, then a foot and more. Everything was cold and wet except his hands, which burned on the heated handlebars that he clung to without gloves, holding on like it was the only thing he knew to do. There was no conscious thought of where he was headed, the road ingrained by decades of muscle memory, intuition, and habit.

He crested the pass and dropped into the head of the valley to the west. The storm made it all like a dream, a dream that faltered with every burst of snow from a busted drift. Then the snowmobile tilted like a boat on water. Tom leaned and pulled and threw his weight until he threw too hard, overcompensated and the sled rolled over and he went under. He felt the weight of the machine on his leg and his arms struggled through powder, grasped at nothing, but he wriggled free. Tried to roll the machine back upright and only sank in the bottomless snow. Felt weak. The cold held him. He didn't know what to do so kept moving. He walked and he walked, feet falling, wheeling along. Knee-deep snow and the blue jeans turned to frozen tubes on his burning skin. The moving kept him just warm enough to feel the cold and the damp and the frozen, which was enough to let him know he was still alive and might stay that way.

When he reached the cabin he had no way of knowing how long he had been moving. He had long since lost feeling in his hands, and his fingers were like clubs fumbling at the latch on the door that was more for bears than anything or anyone else.

Inside, a cold stale single room. The kindling box was filled with ancient dry twigs. How many years since he'd been here? The memories came flooding, thick and gelatinous, muddled as honey dripping from a broken comb. When he got the fire going, he held to it, leaned in and breathed it. Feeling came to his hands in wretched gasps of pain and tears welled in his eyes. Teeth chattered. The warmth was an addiction, he needed it, hated the feeling it gave him. He added some larger pieces and pulled the frozen clothes from his body. Naked and crying he made his way to the stiff mattress bed in the corner made up with wool blankets and stale sheets. Curled up there like a fetus. When the shaking stopped, he fell asleep.

•

Two boys on a hillside play in the sun and the rocks and sage. Heat of an afternoon. The carelessness of summer. On hands and knees, faces close, focused.

You do it, says one.

If you want it so bad why don't you do it?

Don't be a pussy, Tom.

Fuck you, Rust.

Tom tilts the grasshopper, rolling the body between his fingers. A red liquid seeps out of its mouth.

It's bleeding, says Rust.

No it's not. They just do that. It smells really bad. It's a defense mechanism.

You don't even know what that word means, says Rust.

Yes I do.

Just do it already.

Alright alright.

Tom takes his free hand and pinches one of the big hind legs and pulls until it separates from the body. He sets the insect on the ground and it struggles and crawls, falling on its side. Then it is upright and it leaps in spastic desperation. The hop sends it spinning and it tries again but only spins, circling, aimless.

The boys grow bored and walk up to the house. The afternoon is clear and bright and hot, the dry heat of a high desert on the edge of the mountains.

You're sick, says Rust.

What?

You like torturing things. That's like something a serial killer would do.

You're the one who told me to do it.

If I told you to jump off a cliff would you do that?

Don't be a asshole.

What?

Tom walks faster. A gap opens between him and Rust.

What's your problem? says Rust.

Tom says nothing. Walks faster.

Green

The Lutheran pastor Morris Green stared at the crucifix on the wall. Hands rested on the desk. The depiction of the Son of God was lifelike, well proportioned, and white skinned. Small painted nails protruded from his hands and the spot where his feet met. Blood streamed down the cheeks. There were gashes on his torso where Green assumed the whips had struck him on his long, laborious trial. And his eyes were open, staring straight back. *Jeeesus Christ*, thought Green. Then aloud, Our Lord and Savior.

There was no one to hear the pastor's blasphemous thought, nor the feigned correction. No one but the Man Himself, and Green had long since begun to question whether his God was listening, if he cared or was even present in the first place.

A knock on the door startled him and Green gathered the papers before him, a draft of the upcoming Sunday's

sermon he was working on. The theme was on finding ful-
fillment in God's plan, even when all one could see was
discontent. So far he had three sentences on paper. Pushed
it aside. Said, It's open.

The door creaked and pushed inward and a woman
Green did not know and had not seen before in his church
stepped through the opening.

The first thing Green noticed about the woman was
that she was very attractive. Her curly blonde hair and
plump cheeks. An ample bosom, notable even beneath the
heavy gray coat she wore. The curve of her legs in jeans
that clung tight to her thighs. Pastors were not supposed
to notice these things.

Please. Have a seat.

Green had stood and motioned to the chair on the
other side of his desk. The pastor wore clothes fit for any
casual occasion, nothing to identify his position in the
church. Clean crisp jeans and a green plaid button-down
shirt tucked in at the waist where a plain black leather belt
wrapped just below the top of his hips. He adjusted his
glasses that sat on a medium-sized nose beneath dark hair
with strands of gray that were only visible under close in-
spection. An analog watch with a thin leather strap around
his wrist. The woman sat and Green followed suit. As she
lowered her body into the chair, Jesus on his cross returned
to Green's field of vision. He clasped his hands on his lap.

What can I do for you?

The woman looked up. Made eye contact. Green saw the kindness there and the color that was neither green nor brown yet somehow evoked both colors at the same time. More forbidden thoughts flashed across his mind.

Sorry to barge in on you like this, she said. I hope this is a good time.

It's always a good time, said Green. I don't believe we've met. I'm Pastor Green. Most people call me Morris. Or Green.

He held out a hand and it hung in the space between them until she looked at it and raised her own hand to shake. Her grip was strong but not firm, her skin soft.

Oh I'm sorry, she said. My name is Deb Lindholm. I'm the head nurse at Cottonwood Estates. The assisted living facility down in Bonfisk?

Ah, yes, said Green. The Home.

Yes, that's the place. Though I don't necessarily like that name. Too many negative connotations.

Excuse me, said Green, blushing. I didn't mean to offend. I've just heard it called that.

Yes, said Deb. No need to apologize. That is what people call it. For better or worse.

Well, what brings you here today, Deb?

I suppose you heard about Pastor Wiggins, of the Episcopal church? That he's passed on?

No, said Green. I was unaware, though I am sorry to hear it. Must be a great loss for that community.

Yes, and ours as well, said Deb. He was the chaplain who came around every month to visit with some of our more devout residents, which leaves us with a bit of a hole to fill.

Ah, said Green.

Yes, I suppose you've guessed by now why I'm here. You have a good reputation as a kind and giving man.

Green leaned back in his chair. Stretched his arms and clasped his fingers over his head. Returned them to his lap.

Well, I appreciate that, but I'm not Episcopalian. I'm not sure it would be proper.

Oh, neither are most, or perhaps any, of our residents. Most of them just want someone to talk to. Say a blessing. They are approaching the close of their time on earth and they have a lot of time to think about God and life and death and all of that kind of stuff.

Hmm. I don't know.

Well I just hope you'll think about it. It pays, if that's an issue. Or an enticement.

Green shook his head, mouthed a soft, defensive *No, no.*

Three hundred a visit, once or twice a month. Don't matter if you sit with one or twenty, the pay is the same. And there's opportunity for a little more work through the hospice folks, if you want it.

Green quit the defensiveness. He made a modest living as the head of the Lutheran church there, a small house where he lived, basically free of charge, but modesty had its shortcomings.

If you could just think about it. I'm stopping by the Southern Lutheran and the Congregational churches on my way home. See if I can't track down their preachers or pastors or whatever you call them. I wasn't raised in any church so you'll have to excuse my ignorance.

Not at all, said Green. Truth told, I'm not entirely sure what they're called either. Probably pastors.

Deb smiled. Said she had to be going. Green stood and showed her to the door. Shook that soft hand one last time and watched her head down the stairs. Returned to his desk. He leaned back in his chair and saw Jesus staring, still on the cross. Green looked away. Thought about moving that damn crucifix then heard the door to the church open and footsteps climb the stairs, heavier than the sound of the woman's who had just left, more methodical perhaps. Or more tired. A knock on the frame and a head appeared, hair mussed from a hat that had just been pulled. Heavy jacket and a gold badge that read MARSHAL.

Officer, said Green. Please.

Motioned to the chair across, likely still warm from that part of the woman's body that Green was ashamed to be yet could not stop thinking about.

How goes, Father? said the marshal.

I'm fine. Though I'm not a father. How're you, Luke?

Sorry about that. Force of habit. Raised Catholic, you know?

The marshal paused before continuing.

I'm good enough, he said.

They sat. The marshal's eyes wandered. Looked at the walls. Books on the shelf behind the pastor. At last Green could take the silence no longer.

What can I do for you, Luke?

Well, it's not great news. I'll say that much.

Green said nothing. Rested his hands on the desk, leaned in a little.

Does the name Gus Hawkins mean anythin to you?

Green paused. No, he said. I don't believe it does.

Hmm, said Luke. Well, he's a local boy. I thought maybe he could be a member of your church. Don't know why I thought that. Maybe his family was or somethin, or his daddy maybe. Rust Hawkins. Local kid, well not a kid any-more, but anyway, cut to the chase. It's the boy's father, Rust.

The marshal appeared uncomfortable. He fidgeted in his chair then settled before he said, He turned up dead a few days ago. Can't say nothin else bout it so please don't ask.

I'm sorry to hear that.

So'm I, or well, I guess I would be, for the boy's sake, but knowin their history it might not be such a bad thing.

Green was almost offended at the marshal's blunt hon-esty. Gave no outward indication of his thought process. The marshal went on.

Still, there's the boy. He's twelve. No other family in the

valley. Relatives are out of touch. I guess he'll go into foster care or somethin. He's down at the station with Edna
right now. He's stayin with me for the time bein. I went
and picked him up the mornin his dad turned up dead.
Neighbor got worried when his daddy's truck was gone for
a spell. Been fendin for himself I guess.

That's terrible. Is he alright?

Hard to say. He don't talk much. Got some bruises.
Could be nothin. Maybe.

Green leaned back in his chair. Took a deep breath.
Well, he said, what can I do to help?

Well, maybe nothin. I wasn't sure if they was some kind
of support through the church here to help out a little fella
in need.

I don't know, said Green. I could ask around with some
of the families. There's no official system. There's adoption,
but I don't know that that's what you're looking for at this
point, and besides, it's through the central office in Denver. Odds are he'd end up somewhere else. Could be best
for him to stay here, where his home is.

The marshal nodded. Could be, he said.

There was a longer gap. The marshal looked around.
Said, Well, I don't want to keep you.

He slid back in his chair and stood. Green remained
seated.

If you think of somethin you let me know, will you?

Of course I will, said Green.

Then the man was gone. Green, the pastor, alone in his office with his thoughts and the lingering gaze of his one true God. He shook his head. Put on his coat and walked into the bright cold January day.

Green

Green couldn't say why he did it. Maybe it was pure impulse. Maybe it was the eyes of the man on the crucifix staring him down, but any judgment or instruction he gleaned from those eyes he put on himself. He knew that, though wouldn't that be the way God operated? He couldn't say anymore how God operated or why he chose to do it in the way that he did, and there were still other questions that had only begun to metastasize, that he had not yet allowed himself to ask. Whatever the case, he did not have a clear reason for why he was standing in the marshal's office with the child, Gus, before him, but he was.

Green had slept on it, of course. He was not a rash man. Had come to distrust impulse, though on occasion something would stick in his mind and he knew action would need to be taken. By the morning following the marshal's visit in the rectory, Green knew what he would do.

That's not exactly what I meant, said the marshal, standing beside the boy.

I know, said Green, but I got to thinking. God asks us to serve others. I have time. I have a spare room. Could be a temporary thing until a viable permanent option comes up.

The marshal looked at the boy. No indication of whether or not he liked the idea or was even paying attention.

I called the lady down at social services, said the marshal. She's lookin for a foster home. Was maybe goin to come pick him up tomorrow afternoon and take him home with her. I'll see what she says but I'm not opposed to it. What do you think, Gus?

Gus Hawkins looked up. The lump of a greenish bruise adorned his forehead above his right eye. His gaze jumped from marshal to pastor. Back to the floor. He shrugged.

I don't know, said the boy.

Would you be opposed to goin with this man? the marshal asked.

I guess not.

Shrugged again.

Tell you what, said Green. Just come for the night. I've got the day off tomorrow. If you change your mind in the morning we'll find another option.

The boy stared at the floor. Sure, he said.

The marshal patted the kid on the back, a little too hard, and Gus stumbled forward a step.

●

The boy sat at the table. A plate of green beans, half a left-over chicken breast, and canned corn.

Sorry I couldn't get a better meal together, said Green.

Gus pushed the corn around with a spoon. Said nothing.

I'm very sorry about your father. I'm sure he was good man and it probably doesn't make any sense. These things never make sense.

Gus took a bite of chicken breast. Chewed slow. Didn't look up.

I don't know what your religion is, or if you even have one, but my God works in mysterious ways. It can be hard to see the meaning when you're in the thick of it, but the message will be revealed. You just have to have faith.

The words felt hollow as they fell off his tongue. There was very little in his own life that made sense, and his faith had long since been shaken. He felt like a recording. Just hit Play. The same advice he'd been giving for years. Faith, faith, faith. Faith in what? He didn't have an answer to that question anymore, though countless others had come to him as a means to reassure their own.

I'm baptized Catholic, the boy said. First thing he'd said all night.

Well what do you know, said Green. I'm a Lutheran. Those two are related, so to speak.

I've never been to church, Gus went on, still not looking up. My dad said we did it to appease his in-laws and they lied and said my uncle was a fallen Catholic so he could be my godfather but that's not true. He's not Catholic.

Oh, said Green. I see. Well, we've both been baptized so we have that in common.

The boy shrugged. Forked a green bean and lifted it to his mouth.

My dad told me that since my godfather's not Catholic that means I'm damned from the get-go.

Green hesitated. Well, I don't know about all that, he said. My God is pretty forgiving of things that are out of our control.

Still more lies. Seemed to him that the God he'd been preaching about looked for any excuse to shame or judge. Or maybe that was just the parishioners, but then what do the actions of the sheep say about the Shepherd? Then again, wasn't *he* the shepherd? *Forgive me, Father*, he thought.

After dinner he showed the boy to his room. The bathroom. Gave him a towel and encouraged him to shower. Gus seemed to be going through the motions. Green figured that he was in shock. He'd thought that there would be more tears, but the more he thought about it the less he knew what to expect. When Green came in to say good night, Gus was at the bathroom sink and their eyes met in the mirror. Green saw the bruises on the child's back. Big green-brown blotches in random places. Ugly things. Gus made no move to hide or cover or even acknowledge anything, and Green wondered if the boy knew they were there, though how could he not?

If you need anything in the night my room is just down the hall. I'll leave the door open.

Gus nodded. Leaned and spit in the sink. Rinsed.

Sleep in in the morning, said Green. No need to get up early.

Again, the boy nodded. Then Green closed the door. Walked the hall and entered his own room. He did not sleep well that night. He fitted and stirred, rose often to pee. He turned the bedside lamp on and tried reading but his mind was too scrambled to focus on anything outside itself. He did not know at what time he fell asleep but when he woke there was daylight in the windows and the lamp was still on, his book askew beside him. There was movement in the house and he jolted up. *The boy.* He had meant to be up before Gus and castigated himself as he rose, brushed his teeth, and threw some clothes on. He found the boy in the kitchen sitting at the table with the box of Cheerios out and a half-empty bowl before him.

Morning, Gus, said Green.

Gus looked up. Back to his cereal.

I see you made yourself at home. That's good. I fully intended to be up early and cook a decent breakfast. My sleep schedule's all messed up.

He shook his head, adjusting to the presence of another human there in his house at this intimate hour. Green had been living alone for longer than he cared to think about and there were habits and mannerisms that even he was unaware of with no one else present to hold him accountable. Gus was quiet. Ate his Cheerios.

They were around the house for the morning. Gus watched television while Green read and worked on his sermon. As he was prepping lunch the doorbell rang. He answered and a woman in blue jeans and a blouse with a manila folder tucked under her arm stood before him.

Pastor Green, she said. My name is Amelia Gomez. I'm the child-welfare liaison from the Office of Health and Human Services at the county. Marshal Tomlinson said he told you I'd be by.

Yes, of course, said Green. Come in.

He ushered her into the kitchen.

I was just making lunch, he said. Would you like a sandwich?

Thank you, but no. I don't think this will take long and I have other places I need to be.

Ms. Gomez opened the folder and arranged the papers before her in an unceremonious, matter-of-fact way. Green sat at attention, forearms pressed to the table.

This, the woman said, sliding a sheet across the table, will grant you a temporary guardianship of Gus. We are beginnin the process of trackin down any relatives who might have a first claim of guardianship, perhaps an aunt or an uncle. Failin that, a grandparent or perhaps a godparent. If none are found or come forward on their own, Gus will pass into the custody of the state.

Foster care, said Green.

Yes. A foster home. We have many great families in the community. We're lucky here. It is not the foster care that you see on TV. It's a small community. Harder for kids to fall through the cracks here.

That's not what I meant, said Green, though he wasn't sure of this.

This, said Ms. Gomez sliding another sheet across, acknowledges that we will be runnin a background check on you. Normally we do that before grantin charge of a minor, but . . . she smiled, extenuatin circumstances.

Green looked at the paper.

Here's a list of phone numbers. Mine is at the top. Call anytime, day or night. Below that is a list of emergency contacts and other local resources. I've been in touch with the school. They know about the situation and won't expect Gus in class before next Monday at the earliest, though of course he can take as much time as he needs. It will be up to you to communicate with the school for as long as Gus is in your care.

Green stared at the papers. Nodded.

There's just one last thing before I go.

What's that?

Let's go talk to Gus.

The two stood and went into the living room where Gus sat on the couch. He looked up when they came into the room.

You mind if we shut the TV off for a minute? Green asked. This lady here wants to talk to you.

Gus grabbed the remote from the coffee table and hit the Power button. Stared at the two adults.

Hi, Gus, said Ms. Gomez. My name is Amelia. I'm just here to check on you and Mr. Green and see how you're doin. You mind if I sit down?

She hesitated, though did not wait for a response that seemed unlikely to come. Green half leaned on the dresser where the TV sat.

How you doin, Gus?

Gus fidgeted. Said, Fine.

Okay, said Amelia. Well, Mr. Green here has offered to let you stay with him for a while. How would you like to stay here? It's not forever, mind, but it could be for a little while. You think you could be comfortable here?

Gus only shrugged. Green and Amelia made eye contact.

There's nothing required, Green chimed in. You're welcome for as long as you'd like, but you don't have to stay here. If you want, Ms. Gomez can help find someone for you to stay with. Maybe a house with some other children in it.

More fidgeting. It's okay, he said. I can stay here.

I was hopin for a more resoundin yes, said Ms. Gomez, nudging Gus playfully. He didn't say anything, maybe blushed a little.

Well, she said, looking back at Green, that's good enough for me. Just one more thing I need, she said, looking at the boy.

Green tensed without thinking. The boy with the same morose lack of expression.

I need you to give me a hug, she said, and she coaxed the boy to his feet and wrapped him in her arms. Green saw her to the door and thanked her for coming. She said she'd be in touch and not to hesitate if he needed anything. She drove away. Green turned to look at the boy, who was still standing in the spot where the woman had hugged him. Gus watched out the window as the car disappeared. Looked at Green, at his feet. Green wondered what to say. After a prolonged silence in which no ideas came to him, at last he said, You hungry?

Marshal Tomlinson

*H*ere's the thing about this job. I'd like to say I got into law enforcement because of noble intentions of protectin people and justice and whatnot, but when it comes down to it, it was just a job, or that's how I felt at the time. A town like this, law enforcement is pretty simple. Borin by some people's standards, though I never found it to be like that. I keep busy enough. Every once in a while somebody gets drunk and you got to take em in and let em cool off. They go home the next day. Judge assigns some community service over the matter and we all move on. Aside from that it's mostly minor infractions. Parkin violations. A loose dog or two or ten. Of course there is the occasional domestic dispute. Can't say I enjoy that aspect of the work. Especially since more often than not I know the folks. Feels like an intrusion into their personal lives. Of course since they called me in the first place I suppose I shouldn't feel that way, but it can't be helped. Then sometimes you help someone get out of an abusive situation. Suppose I ought to feel good about that, but I never do. That's the thing about a town this size. Somethin happens and odds are damn near guaranteed that you know the people involved. And that's hard. Makes you feel a little dirty, like you're always sweepin up after folks or helpin them sweep it under the rug, or keepin em from doin so. Everythin's bound to get messy and personal. Take for instance this one family a while back. Again, I won't say who cause they're still around. Both of em work in emergency response and have for years. I believe that's how they met. Anyway, a call goes out one night. Head-on collision out 105. Maybe ten miles down highway. Drunk driver. Lord knows what he was doin drivin in the wrong lane but there he was. Front corners of the vehicles clipped and they both spun around and the other one landed upside down in the ditch. Like I said, call goes out. Can't recall now who phoned it in. Probly someone come up on the accident. Musta been. Anyhow, call goes out. This couple, friends of mine, they head out on call. Their son, sixteen, new driver, was out with friends. It's a weekend and he's still not home. It's pretty late but they don't think much of it. Still, there's a little worry that nestles down in their gut and they push it aside like they've learned to do over the years. You don't think about those things when you're goin out on a call, otherwise you wouldn't never make it out. But they get out there. The drunk guy is wanderin down the shoulder, barely a scratch on im. Happens more often than you'd think. They *go limp or somethin and the intoxication kinda helps them come through the trauma, even though it was the cause of it in the first place. Then the dad looks down in the ditch. Recognizes the car there. Doesn't see a face or even most of the body. Just a shoe. Somethin as small and familiar as that, and he knows. DOA. Probly died on impact. He just stood there starin, not sayin a word till somebody who knew what was goin on took him by the shoulders and guided him away. Can't watch a thing like that. Nuff to break a man. And you think to yourself,* What are the odds? That the guy would find his own kith and kin in a head-on accident in the middle of the night? *That's my point. A town this size it's not really all that far-fetched. I'd go as far to say it's bound to happen sooner or later. They say the truth is stranger than fiction. I say bullshit. I think some people just have a hard time acceptin the truth so they say somethin like that to make it seem unbelievable. I say the truth makes sense, typically. If you look at all the factors that went into its makin, you can usually connect the dots. What's that sayin about the simplest solution almost always bein the correct one? Most days that proves true, or that's what I thought, anyhow. Now I'm not so sure. There are things in this world that happen outside the realm of reason, and it can drive a person mad just tryin to make any sense of it. Then again, could be I'm just havin a hard time acceptin the truth of this matter.*

Couple days after the body of Rust Hawkins turned up we

took some snowmobiles up to the Horak family ranch. Me, both my deputies, and a couple folks from the Mountain Rescue team. Place was abandoned. Seems to have been for years. I heard a while back that Tom Sr. had gone over the hill. Hadn't taken too long after the missus passed on. Happens that way in a long marriage. You depend on each other in intangible ways. Tom Jr. does not appear to have taken on the family trade. Windows boarded up at the house. Snowdrifts trapped the barn door shut. Rusted machinery growin icicles like a fungus. I just kind of stood there for a while in the quiet. Looked up at the hills. Nowhere logical to go yet a million places he coulda gone. Snowmobile was reported missin from the trailhead where the trucks were found. Could be Tom took it. Where to? Who knows? Storm like that there aint no trackin nothin. I say the odds of him still breathin at this point are slim to nil. Probly turn up when the snow melts, if he turns up at all. Maybe years from now someone'll find a piece a clothin or somethin. That happens. Best we can hope for at this point, my opinion. Still . . . I don't know. Don't sit right, but then, how could it?

Tom

Tom grumbled awake through a fading dream. Something from his childhood. Dream or memory, he wasn't sure. His body ached, every inch of it. There was some warmth beneath the blankets, but the air was cold. He could see his breath. Stretched one leg out and recoiled when he encountered a roughness and something that was not him moved beneath the blankets. He yelped and rolled out of the bed, pulling a mess of sheets and blankets with him, and saw the mouse emerge and flee across the cabin floor.

Tom pulled himself from the bedding and as he did he felt the stiffness in his joints from his trek into the mountains. His hips locked up and his shoulders ached from throwing around the heavy snowmobile.

He was naked, his lanky body pale and hairy in all the normal places, though not excessively so. He was a skinny man. Bones protruded from the skin at abrupt angles. Shoulder blades jutted out like underdeveloped bat wings.

He found his clothes in a lump beside the woodstove. The outside of the pile had dried, though most of the fabric remained wet. He got a fire kindled through chattering teeth and numbing extremities. When the orange glow roared with oxygen, he shut the little black door and hovered over the heat like a gargoyle. Hung the clothes from chairs that he pulled from the table in the corner and wrapped himself in a blanket that he shook out hard and thorough before draping it over his shoulders and pulling it tight at his chest. Knees tucked in so his body was a ball, as he did when he was a child, the opening of the blanket cracked to the heat. He stayed that way until the room had warmed and his breath disappeared and the panic of the cold had left him.

The cabin was a small one-room number, plywood floors painted a drab grayish blue. Walls of unpainted plywood and a modest line of countertop and cabinetry. Sink without a faucet. The table and the bed. Window wet with melting frost. Tom rose and went to the window. The bit of moisture blurred the view but he could see that the storm had broken. The world a blanket of white.

He dressed. The clothes wrinkled and stiff, as if starched. Snow had drifted in around the door and when he opened it he could see no sign of footprints from his arrival. It was late in the day, the blue of twilight, half-moon showing itself high in the sky. The snow level was above his boots as he waded around back of the cabin to the shed that was built off the wall. Snow fell in along his calves and began to melt. Inside the shed split wood was stacked against the aged slats where white light crept in through the cracks. A few implements. Axe and maul. Splitting wedges. A flat shovel and the hooks they'd used to stack bales of hay when they'd come with animals.

The cabin belonged to Tom's family. Technically it was an old mining claim passed down through the generations. An inholding surrounded by national forest land, it sat high in the mountains above the valley that held the family ranch. No one had ever mined on the property and likely never would. More of a practical designation that allowed a prior generation to build the cabin. Tom, an only child, and his father and mother had used it as an escape in the summer and to hunt out of in the fall. He wondered how many people might know about this cabin and if anyone would come looking for him here. He thought there were few and the chances were slim, counted on it even. His father's secrecy around hunting spots led him to be vague in its description whenever possible.

As Tom gathered a load of split rounds of Doug fir, a wash of remembrance came over him. Visions of his younger days. His father, bearded and dressed in wool and canvas sitting in a chair out front with a hand-rolled cigarette and a glass of whiskey and water on an evening in autumn. Always the whiskey. His mother on horseback in sun-faded jeans and a cotton T-shirt, smiling at him as he watched her come in from a ride from his perch in the slanted limbs of a dead snag that leaned against another tree on the edge of the timber. Sadness welled at the thought of his mother. Things he wished he knew about her and never would. Opportunities lost to time that would not return. A slip of anger at the image of his father. Things he wanted to say that the man would never hear.

Tom came back to the cabin, his arms loaded with firewood, and a breeze came in through the door at his back. He spent the evening melting water on the woodstove and sifting mouse turds from a package of pasta he found in a cabinet. Cooked it down and threw in a can of black beans and ate his fill.

Green

A moth fluttered around the hole in the top of the lampshade on Morris Green's bedside table. There was silence, then the muffled skitter of powdered wings struggling against cloth and heat. Green sat and did not move. He was thinking about the following morning and what it might bring. The boy would be returning to school and he was going to drop him off and after he would go into the office to speak with the school counselor, possibly others in the administration. Rationally he did not think there was anything to be apprehensive about. Irrationally he heard the fey voices of judgment come down upon his shoulders like so many bricks.

The boy is living with a pastor? A grown man, alone? What could he possibly want with a child?

He knew the stereotypes, and who could blame them? How many hundreds, if not thousands, of years of precedence? A few bad apples. He knew better, though. It was more like a mixed cargo of semi-rotten fruit, not all bad but every piece is tainted. Regardless of how many years he'd served in this community, Green knew he could not escape people's preconceived notions, nor did he feel he needed to. He wasn't even Catholic but knew that didn't matter. A single man, old, well, older. Hell, if pressed on the subject he wasn't sure he could give an explanation as to what his motivations were. It was a feeling, a feeling that this was what he needed to do and that the reasons would shake out in the long run, but he also knew that would not be enough for most people. Just wished he did not have to deal with any of it, but he also could not hide. That would make matters worse.

Downstairs in the kitchen, moonlight spilled through unshaded windows. The white midnight world glowed as he filled a glass of cold water and stood drinking in a white T-shirt, striped undershorts, and slippers. Sipped water and watched the street. It was like watching a photograph. Nothing moved. Nothing changed. Time froze and slipped at random intervals. The clock told him he had been there for nearly an hour. He climbed the stairs with as little sound as possible. Even so the old house squealed and creaked beneath the weight of him.

In the dark hallway of the second floor, he stood for a long time. One window at the end by the entrance to the boy's room and some moonlight leaked up from the floor below at the top of the stairs. Slow footsteps down the hall to the window. Stood looking out. Closed his eyes. Listened.

The sound of his breath was a slow constant. Occasional squeak if he shifted his weight. And beneath it, behind the door, the unmistakable sound of a child weeping.

Green stood for a long time, now afraid that Gus would hear him. He felt a mix of wanting to comfort the boy and not wanting to infringe on his sense of privacy. At least the boy was grieving, he thought. He'd been worried when Gus did not appear out of sorts in his first days of coming to live with him. He'd thought the child would be distraught, but then what did he know about loss, or children? His own parents were still alive and well in Michigan. They'd come out for Christmas last year.

Back in bed, Green lay in the dark. His eyes adjusted to the light. Watched the shadows. Woke to the sound of his alarm. There would be no sleeping late this morning.

Gus woke of his own accord. Green was grateful for his self-sufficiency in this regard. He was uncomfortable entering into those more intimate moments with him, such as the very beginning and end of the day.

They arrived at school to the chaos of parents and children unloading cars and entering the building. Most were preoccupied with their own affairs and paid little attention to the pastor and the boy. Green was surprised by how few people he recognized. Even in a town as small as this there were a variety of social circles, it seemed.

Gus ran off toward his classroom. *Kids know what to do*, thought Green. *Thank God for that.* He walked down the hall as the bell rang and crowds cleared. A few straggling students running late and parents rushing back out the doors to get to work on time, or not. He made his way to the central office.

Mr. Green, said a woman he did not recognize. Cathy's waiting for you. Just back there.

She motioned to a short hallway behind her desk with a variety of doors, only one of which was open. Through the open door he found a woman sitting behind a desk, brown curly hair pulled back and a loose-fit sweater drooped off her torso. She looked up from a computer screen as he stepped through the doorway.

Mr. Green, please come in. Have a seat.

Thank you. He sat in a chair opposite the woman with her desk between them. She clasped her hands, leaned back.

I appreciate you reaching out, she said.

Yes. I just wanted to introduce myself. I don't know that there is anything specific we need to talk about. Just seems that given the circumstances we ought to have a little communication between us.

Absolutely. I guess first off I'd like to know, is there anything you need from me pertaining to Gus's well-being?

Green thought. No, he said. I don't think so. Or not that I can think of. Ms. Gomez covered a lot of it.

Good. She's great, isn't she?

Green agreed. Folded his hands on his lap then separated them and set them on the armrests of the chair.

I guess, he said, I had a similar question for you. Is there anything you need from me pertaining to Gus and school?

Not specifically, she said. Hesitated, then, Are you aware of Gus's behavioral issues?

Green donned a look of genuine concern. No, he said. I'm afraid I'm not.

The counselor leaned back in her chair and took a breath. Gus can be prone to outbursts, she said. He has some trouble managing his anger, not unusual for a boy of his age, but Gus seems to have more anger than the other boys.

Well, that's understandable, given what I know of his background.

Understandable, yes, but it can cause problems at school and with other children.

I would imagine it does. The boy seems to be kind of a loner, but it's hard for me to tell if that's just a product of what he's going through.

I'd say that's a fair assessment. He'll seek attention from the other boys on occasion but he often keeps to himself.

Green didn't say anything. He wasn't sure what could be accomplished from this conversation, but it was good to know a little more about Gus's situation at school and before the . . . incident. Green found it difficult even to think about naming what had happened when he tried to imagine what the boy had gone and was continuing to go through.

And, Cathy went on, there is the question of actual schoolwork. Gus will need time to get back on his feet. We all understand that, and a lot of assignments will more than likely go undone. There's nothing wrong with that. But if he starts to fall behind on the skills he needs to be on par with the other children, it's going to get complicated.

I suppose you're correct there, said Green, not sure where the conversation was going.

It's going to take some work to keep him on track. There is only so much that can be accomplished during school hours. The children who excel the most have help at home from parents. Or guardians, she added.

Yes, of course.

Green had not thought of this. There was a lot to raising a child that had never crossed his mind, no experience to plant it there.

He's doing fine for now but if we get into early March or even late February and he's not able to keep up with the workload, there are going to be consequences to his education. We'll do everything we can to help him, but it's going to take some extra effort on your and Gus's parts.

I understand, Green said, questioning whether he really did or not.

Cathy looked at her watch. I have another appointment here in a few minutes. I'm glad that we met. If there is anything you need from me, you know where to find me.

I will. Thank you.

And if Gus is having a hard time with anything, you give me a call and I'll make sure we can provide some extra support.

Green walked out through the empty halls. A few glimpses of school life through narrow mesh-lined windows on heavy doors. The day was sunny. He drove across town on snow-packed roads and made his way to the church and pulled up on the street out front. The engine on his Subaru Legacy ticked as it cooled and he sat in the car and did not want to move. It was a funny little car. Green was not much of a car person, no real interest in machines in general, but even he felt emasculated in this thing, though it handled the wintry roads just fine and had been provided by the church when he'd taken the job some years back. He did not complain, not outwardly anyhow. But something about it left him unsatisfied, like he'd been allowing someone else to determine his quality of life. He laughed. *Quality of life.* He wasn't sleeping on the street. He had a car. One that he didn't have to pay for. Funny, he thought, how you can convince yourself how bad you have it. He thought of that nurse from the old folks' home and smiled. He had to call her to set up his first visit. Had been putting it off, nervous somehow. Or maybe excited. It was hard to tell the difference sometimes. Better to get it over with. He stepped out of the car and went into the church.

Tom

The moose, antlerless and long legged, did a slow step through the snow that would have easily come to a man's thigh. It paused. Sniffed at the air and looked about. Sank its muzzle in the snow, pushed the white to one side then the other, flicked it out ahead. Dove again and emerged with yellowed strands of dead grass dangling out the corner of its mouth. Tom settled the crosshairs on the ribs above a foreleg just behind the shoulder. With the rifle perched on the sill of an open window, the cold air coming in had chilled the space and he was beginning to lose feeling in his fingers. Hunger like a stabbing gut ache. The feeling had set in a few days after arriving at the cabin. More than a week had gone by since then, perhaps longer. It was probably early February, but he couldn't be sure of the exact date. His breath rising through the cold breeze, he drove out the sensations

SALVATION

of his body. Focused on the animal in the view of the scope. Watched the black lines of the crosshairs rise and settle with his breath, the blurred pines in the distance. Touched the trigger.

•

THERE IS THE FATHER. THE BOY, TOM, ON THE ROCK
outcropping watches the cow elk and calf wander on a
slope across the draw. He is long in watching the animals
through his scope. So long that his father gives nervous
encouragement, watching the dwindling final light of day.
Pulls the trigger and the cow turns and sprints uphill.
Collapses in a gully and gives a gargled moan. The calf,
confused and terrified, lingers a moment then bolts in the
opposite direction.

She's dyin, his dad says.

Tom's body shakes with adrenaline.

They field dress the animal in the dark. Hang the quarters in a tree and take loads themselves. It is not far to the
cabin. The windows are dark. As they approach, his father
says, That was a close one. Sun was goin down. Thought
you was gonna puss out on me. Slaps his son on the shoulder. Takes a swig of the flask he keeps in his pocket, a constant that evening. Every evening. Yeah, says his father, I
been worried you been goin a little sissy on me, though
your mom don't like it when I say that. I guess you got
more grit than I thought. We'll make a man outta you yet.

The boy says nothing. Feels a mix of shame and pride,
undercurrents of rage. Stares at the faint dark that is the
horizon. At least his father is in a jovial mood, the thrill of
a successful hunt. If things had gone different, well, Tom

doesn't want to think about that. When he lies down to sleep, he is haunted by the memory of the calf running into the trees. Thinks of it now, alone there in the cold and the dark.

●

Tom, exhausted, collapsed on the bed. He'd finished hanging the moose quarters in the woodshed as the sun was setting, having shot the animal in the early morning. Every day he'd sat by the window waiting for something to wander past. So hungry he'd have shot a coyote if given the chance. It was a small moose, as far as moose go, but it would be plenty to see him through what was left of winter. There were a few dry goods and cans left in the cabinet, but he could eat all he wanted of those and still feel like he was starving to death. The nutrients his body lacked. The moose was a godsend. It was late enough in the winter that he didn't have hope of an elk or deer wandering past. Most had migrated to the sage hills south of there, beyond the mountains where the snow did not fall as deep. Perhaps a few lone bulls overwintering in the mountains like legendary hermits. Where they dwelled, he knew not. Moose he knew very little about. Whether it was normal or not for this cow to be milling about he could not say. He was just grateful for it and that was all that he knew.

That night, before a roaring fire hot enough that he shed his clothing and sat naked on a folded blanket, he ate greasy moose loin seasoned only with salt. Licked the melted fat off his fingers and felt more satisfied than he had in weeks. Perhaps it was the clarity that only a full stomach can bring, but he thought, as if for the first time since the beginning of this endeavor, of the boy. Gus.

Gus Hawkins. Rust Hawkins's kid. *Rust.* His mind went back . . .

•

HE AND THE BOY BESIDE A SMALL BEAVER POND IN the wilderness. Sepia light of late-evening quiet. They sit, waiting. For nothing. The sun sets. It grows dark, and still there is quiet. Not silence. It is never silent in the woods. Always the rustling of leaves. Whistle of a breeze. Squirrel chatter. But it is quiet. They eat freeze-dried dinners by the light of headlamps.

I'm sorry we didn't see nothin, says Tom.

Gus slurps a bite of soupy lasagna. That's okay, he says. It's good to be out here.

Tom finishes his meal. A night bird sounds off in the brush somewhere along the far side of the beaver pond. The night is clear, a warm fall. In the morning they rise before the sun and pack up as the woods begin to brighten. They hike with rifles uncomfortable on their shoulders, the man only slightly more graceful at the feat than the child, no matter that the boy has only a .22 brought along to plunk dusky grouse out of tree limbs. The man's is a .30-06 built to take down larger game at a distance or through the heavy brush. A couple more years and Gus will be old enough to go after elk himself. They sit atop the pass and a late-morning wind comes up, the sun on their unshielded faces, and they eat hard cheese and sausage.

Well, says Tom, did you have fun?

Catches the boy with a mouthful. He takes a hard

swallow of unchewed sausage, coughs and sputters out, Oh yeah.

Tom smacks Gus on the back, jests, Don't hurt yourself there, kid.

Gus washes down the chunks with a swig of water.

I'm sorry your dad couldn't make it, says Tom.

Gus is light and easy. He smiles often. They walk down toward the trailhead, both feeling the success of a hunt that did not see a kill. Tom can see it that way, though it is not what his own father would have deemed anything resembling success.

They don't talk much. The boy walks behind and Tom slows his gait, still moving, to appear as though he is not waiting for the child.

At the trailhead is the truck of the father, Rust Hawkins, and here the child's demeanor shifts. It is a subtle thing, but Tom is quick to notice the absence of the smile that so easily graced the young face earlier in the day. They unshoulder their packs. Rust is nowhere to be seen. Minutes pass. They sit on the tailgate and sip water, content in their exhaustion. After a half hour Rust saunters up the road. His walking is slow and lazy, boots scuff the gravel, and he is unkempt.

Well well well, he says. Look who decided to show up.

Rust, says Tom, grimacing as he braces himself for an onslaught. He can tell that Rust is not in a good mood. Has seen the half-empty bottle in the cab of the pickup, sure the boy has seen it as well, though neither acknowledge, an un-spoken resolution between the two. Gus doesn't respond.

Well, says Rust. Where's the elk?

In the woods, says Tom. The boy is silent.

Oh come on, says Rust. Tom Horak, the great white hunter. Empty-handed. I thought this was like your secret spot or somethin. Near guarantee. That's what you said, wasn't it?

I don't think I ever said that.

Rust sticks a hand in his pocket. Rocks from heel to toe on his boots and back again. Picks at something in his teeth with an index finger.

You did, says Rust, then before any further argument can occur, Did you at least learn somethin, boy?

Gus shrugs. Hesitates. I guess, he says. I had fun.

Well, fun don't count for nothin cept in horseshoes and hand grenades.

The three of them stare at each other, at nothing.

I've been waitin around all fuckin mornin for you two. I'm ready to get out of here. Gus, let's get movin.

Tom gets up off the tailgate. Helps Gus push his pack up into the bed of his father's truck.

We'll get one next year, says Tom. You done good though.

He gives Gus a hug and Gus climbs into the cab and shuts the door.

Guess you two are awful close, says Rust.

Tom shrugs. He's a good kid, he says.

Damn right he is. Thanks to me.

Tom shoulders his pack. Makes to leave.

Don't get too used to this, says Rust. I had to work, but it won't always be like that. I'll teach my son to hunt. You want a son, you find yourself a woman and make your own.

Rust watches Tom walk off to his own truck in silence. Oh fuck you, he says just loud enough for Tom to hear, and Tom sits in his cab as he watches in the mirror the jerky way Rust's truck lurches out of the parking lot. A sea of unsavory feelings washes down through his body.

●

Tom felt the same shame guilt anger hate seething out from his core as he sat full of moose meat, a bit of nausea from the introduction of game meat into his system. Lay on his side on the bed, just a blanket over him. He could see the length of his life, frame by frame, as pictures in his mind, everything leading up to this point, the things he did, things he wanted and never got. The abuse at the hands of his father. Something resembling that in the way Rust treated his own son, the boy that Tom had come to love. That was all gone now. Alive only in his memory. Tom saw himself there in that moment, and looking forward, a black void. He could not envision any way forward. Fell asleep, that electricity emanating out from the center of him to the tips of every limb. Woke in the night with a terrible gas, the stench of himself pouring out from beneath the blanket into the cold room. Felt another fart coming on that grew and he knew there was more than foul air behind it. Tearing out into the cold moonless night, he just had time to rip down his wool long underwear and blast hot liquid from his anus onto the surface of the snow, his intestines grumbling and juicy. It would pass. His system would accustom to the moose meat. He just had to bear it for now. Cleaned himself as best he could and stumbled into the relative warmth of the cabin.

Marshal Tomlinson

I come up in these mountains. Raised two boys here. Now they're both grown and gone on to other places, one of em with kids of their own. My wife and I have gone back and forth over the years debatin over whether we prefer the silence or get lonely without all that commotion. We still can't make up our minds about it. When our oldest comes home with his clan the hubbub of bodies and movement and conversation always feels like a godsend. Same goes for the stillness it leaves in its wake.

All those early days of parenthood seem like a dream now. A blur. Maybe it's just the busyness of it all. Perhaps the fog of years. In the silence now I have a lot of time to think. Too much time maybe. More and more now I find myself thinkin about death. Not that I'm focused on it or even close to somethin like obsessed. It's like my mind just goes there without my realizing it.

I'm not so old. Seventy-one. That's old enough I guess.

Old enough that it's not uncommon for folks I've known for a long time to be kickin the bucket. I feel like most people woulda quit worryin about it by now, but I can't help it. One of the reasons I'm still workin. If I retired I'd be a dead man. Sure as shit.

This whole topic used to scare the hell outta me. Just the thought of dyin. All that nothinness. Or maybe not. If I look at life, the things I've witnessed, I'd have to say the odds are in favor of some kind of power greater than us, maybe not pullin strings, but somehow influencin the goins on of the universe from behind the scenes somewhere. Even that don't guarantee no nothin like a afterlife or anythin like that. I aint no fool in that regard.

Now I aint never seen no ghost, but I know people who have. People I know and respect. My wife for instance. Says she seen an old woman one time in her grandmama's house. Standin in the corner. Just looked at her and walked off through a wall and was gone. She swears, and I have no reason to doubt her. I can't say as she's ever lied to me before. Not intentionally nohow. Still, I'm not sure I believe in ghosts. In the possibility of ghosts. Is that a rational thing? To believe the stories of the ones who tell but not believe in the existence of the subject matter of the stories? I guess that's the very definition of irrational. It just don't make no sense. That we would die and then just hang around on the other side of a thin veil that sometimes pokes through? Still gives me a little hope, or somethin resemblin it. That maybe the energy we carry that leaves the body when we, you know, pass on, that maybe it goes somewhere. Does somethin. Then I get to thinkin that's just some comfortin sort of bullshit, a barrier against the unknown. Sweet little denials that keep us from losin our marbles all the goddamn time. I think about it long enough and the old fear comes on, takes hold, and I'm just a little kid, panicked in the middle of the night and runnin like hell to my mother's bedside. That's how I know I aint mastered the concept of my own mortality. Maybe I never will. Maybe that's the point of this life. To spend the entirety of it figurin it out and why we got to move on at all, or short of that, maybe we just have to accept the inevitability of it. I don't know how to do that.

Green

In mid-February a ridge of high pressure settled over the valley. Temperatures plummeted. The coldest troughs of the river bottoms dropped to forty below zero. Temperature inversions stuck the summits of surrounding peaks thirty degrees warmer than the valleys. Ice fog off the lake hung in the air, crystalline and sparkling. Cars were not wont to start and dogs pranced and limped to keep their paws off the frigid ground. Still, life did not grind to anything resembling a halt. The days were growing longer and the sunshine drew folks from their homes. A warming trend throughout the high pressure meant by midafternoon it could be pleasant outside, relatively speaking.

Green drove down valley through one such frigid morning. It was past the hour that most people commuted to work and the roads were dry and empty and he drove with the radio off. A few miles outside of Bonfisk, the basin opened into high-desert sage hills and pasture-land where the cows wintered and fed off bales of hay harvested out of those same fields six or seven months prior.

Town was quiet, not out of the ordinary. He took a side street through the neighborhood, avoiding either of the highways that intersected in the heart of town, to the Home. It was located in a quiet corner near the river on a triple lot with large cottonwoods and a spruce in the yard along the street, which was covered in a few inches of old snow. Bonfisk being down valley, some thirty-plus miles from the true mountains, it got far less precipitation. Green parked on the street and walked inside with a Bible in his left hand.

Two large glass doors led into a foyer with a desk on the right and an open area to the left, sofa with a couple throw pillows and an old recliner centered around a rug. There was good lighting through a few windows and it smelled like a hospital. Green stood and looked around. It was quiet. No one about. Found a silver push bell on the desk and he tapped it with a middle finger. Stood waiting. Moments later Deb appeared, hurried though not frazzled, from a hallway beyond the sofa.

Right on time, she said.

Green smiled. I'm nothing if not prompt.

Well, let me just do one thing and I'll give you the grand tour.

Deb disappeared into a small room behind the desk with the bell. Green heard some rummaging and Deb reemerged.

Alright. They left the lobby area and walked down a hallway. How was the drive?

Very pleasant.

The halls were empty. Late morning. A series of doors, open or closed. This hall teed into another and they hung a left.

This is the cafeteria back here. Not sure why I'd show you that other than it's there. If you're ever hungry, we can usually scrounge something up. And back here—they'd turned around and headed the opposite direction—is the TV room. It was a small room, smaller than the lobby, with couches and recliners and folding chairs leaned against the wall. Three senior citizens watched a news channel in silence.

That's more or less it, said Deb. The rest of the place is just rooms. Well, not just. But here, let me get you the list.

They returned to the lobby and Deb went into the little office. Came out with a sheet of paper.

Here are room numbers and names. I crossed out the ones who aren't any kind of religious.

Green took the list and looked it over. He read the names

and numbers, peeked in a few rooms to find the slumbering elderly. Could not help but think of death. A couple closed doors. Then an open door and a woman sitting in a chair with a book on her lap. Green stood in the doorway and tapped on the frame. The woman startled. Had been dozing. She blinked awake and gazed at him through watery eyes. She looked very old. Perhaps in her upper eighties or early nineties. Had that lost look that some old people have. Green wondered about the state of her mind.

Twila, he said. I'm Pastor Green. Is this a good time?

Oh, yes. Fumbled the book closed and set it on the bedstand beside the chair below a plain blue lamp. I guess I dozed off and that's a fact. Deborah said you would be comin in today and I wanted to be presentable when you came.

Green took in the rest of her appearance. A clean white blouse and buttoned sweater with pleated pants. Gleaming shoes. Toe-pointed flats. Something you might wear to church, a nice supper perhaps. She wore reading glasses and she removed them and set them on the book.

Good book?

Oh I don't know. I can't hardly make it through a page before I doze off. Some people stop sleepin in their older age. Not me though. Or maybe I'm past that point. When the end is nigh you start to sleep a lot. I've seen that. She stared at him.

May I come in? Green was still standing in the doorway.

Oh of course. Where are my manners? She made to stand.

No, no. Don't get up. There's no need for formality.

Well just come on in then. There's a chair there, you can have a seat. She motioned to a straight-backed wooden chair pulled into a small desk on the wall. It's not very comfortable but these rooms are so small. That's all I really have the space for.

Green pulled the chair out and spun it around so he faced the woman. She sat there staring at him. I'm Twila Rogers. Shoulda said that sooner. I forget sometimes. Just little things.

That's alright.

Well I don't think so, but what can you do. Past a certain age your mind starts to get muddled, or at least mine has. She paused. Took a deep breath and looked in his eyes. It's frustratin.

I can only imagine.

I hope so. You're a nice young man, or, well, younger than me by a fair bit. I guess if we're lucky we live long enough for our minds to go. Though quite a few folks have differin opinions on that, my husband one of em. I suppose he felt lucky to bow out before he had to deal with any of this nonsense. Well, I know he did. Always said if he ever got to where he was in diapers or didn't know who he was he wanted me to take im out back and shoot im. Heart attack did that for me. I guess that's a good thing though I think he was jokin. About the takin im out back and shootin im part.

Everything's in God's plan I suppose.

Twila wobbled her head from side to side. Looked skeptical. I suppose it is. What else could it be? Though it can be hard at times to see the plan. I guess that's the point though. Why it's called *faith*? Not *proof*?

Yes. I'd say that's a good way to think of it.

Then sometimes I think life is all the proof we need.

How do you mean?

This life. She paused and Green thought she had lost her train of thought again. She gathered herself and turned serious. This life is a miracle. And I expect death'll be no differnt.

Oh?

Well don't you think so? I've seen things in this life that defy explanation. The simple existence of such a thing as this life. That's my proof.

Life is full of little miracles. We just have to slow down and pay attention.

His words felt hollow.

That's not what I'm talkin about. Twila had turned serious again. Pointed her finger at him, her hand shaking without intention. I'm talkin about real, honest-to-God, turnin-the-water-into-red-wine miracles. They exist.

Such as?

Well, childbirth for one. Some women disagree, and

maybe I do too, to an extent. It's a hellacious mess when you get down to it, but the fact that a woman can go through that and come out the other side and with a little baby to boot? Gotta be some kinda higher power involved if you ask me. You ever seen it?

What? Childbirth?

Hell yes childbirth. Aint you listenin?

Can't say I have. Seen it.

Why not? You Lutherans are allowed to procreate, aint ya? Not like those teetotalin Catholics. The priests anyhow. The rest of em seem to do nothin but fornicate.

Twila donned a look of disgust and shook her head in short, terse jerks. Green sat there, not knowing what to say. After a while, he asked, Are you afraid of death?

Twila smiled. Regained that absent-minded serenity.

Oh no. I suppose it will come as a relief. The longer you go on livin, the more difficult it gets. The one thing that scares me, though, is I don't know what it's goin a feel like. I just hope it don't hurt.

Some people say it's just like going to sleep.

Ya, well, anyone who's describin what death feels like aint gone through with it themselves, and that's a fact.

I suppose you're right about that.

I am right. But the relief don't come from knowin what it will feel like or even what's goin a happen after. It's knowin that you won't have to go through any of this suffern no more.

I'm sorry life has gotten that way for you.

She batted her hand through the air.

Name me one religion that says life is just peaches and cream. Everybody's lookin forward to some grand paradise after death. Fluffy clouds and virgins and enlightenment. Everybody's goin a be there, even the damn dog. I'm not sure I believe in all that. It's too gaudy. God's not gaudy.

Green thought about the pun there. Smiled. Twila was all business.

What do you think will happen then?

She shrugged. How should I know?

It seems you've been thinking about it. Any theories?

Well of course I've been thinkin bout it. How could I not?

That's not what I meant.

I know I know. I'm sorry. It's gettin on toward lunch. I get cranky when I'm hungry.

Green looked at the digital clock on the bedstand. Read 10:30 a.m.

God's in you and me and everyone else and that's a fact. Don't you agree?

I do.

Well I think when we die we tap into some kind of greater consciousness. A God consciousness, if you will. Like a raindrop slippin through the surface of a river? Then it's just part of that river, completely indiscernible, no differnt than any other bit of that water. All the little individuals makin up the whole. If God is in us, then we are in God and there's no separation. And things go on as they have for eternity. Perhaps we'll live again in some form. Not necessarily reincarnation, but maybe.

I can't say I have a Bible passage to support what you're talking about.

There's a lot of good stuff in there, but it don't cover everythin. Lot of nonsense too. All those *begat*s and *be-got*s and the incest. I guess that's what a lot of humanity is though, lots of senseless breedin.

That's kind of Old Testament stuff. What you're talking about?

Is that not part of the book? That's the problem with people. We want to disregard the parts that make us uncomfortable. You know there are places in the world where slavery still goes on? How you supposed to reckon with somethin like that? Little girls gettin treated like whores. Boys too. All that evil. She gave Green a stern sideways look.

There has always been evil in the world.

That's right. Prolly always will be. Maybe that's why everyone's lookin forward to the next life.

Are you? Looking forward to it?

I try to stay focused on this one. It can be hard in a place like this. Everyone's sort of right on the edge. Nature of the game, I suppose. You don't see any young folk in here. I guess that's a good thing.

Green did not respond. After a moment Twila looked uncomfortable. Fidgeted in her chair.

I guess I've taken enough of your time. Plus I need to see a man about some flowers. She winked at him.

Ah, well. It was very nice talking with you. Should we pray?

Oh you're too kind. Nothin fancy, please. A simple Our Father will do.

Green said the words, his mind wandering. The prayer had become routine over the years, and he did not need to think. He couldn't quite match the woman's cheeriness with her fixation on death. Maybe he just didn't quite understand what it's like to be that close to the end. He hoped he didn't have to think about it. Truth was he was afraid of death. Not just the act of dying and what may or may not come next but the physical presence of it. This place stank with it. It had been a while since he'd been around it, not since his grandparents had passed a decade or more prior, and he only hoped it was something a body could get used to.

Green left Twila sitting in her chair with the book on the bedstand. Walked down the hall to a room with a cracked door. The name on the placard matched the one from his list: Thomas Horak. He knocked. Pushed the door open and saw a man in a white gown on a bed with an oxygen mask over his face. He appeared to be sleeping.

Green stepped into the room. Pulled a chair out from the desk in the corner and sat. He watched the man who he knew was not really sleeping because Deb had told him about this Mr. Horak. No longer present in this world. Not yet passed on. He looked at the chart.

Says here you're a Catholic, Mr. Horak. I'm Lutheran. Generally speaking, most Catholics are okay with that. Seems to be a theme in my life right now. Wayward Catholics. I'm guessing you're nonpracticing at this point?

He felt bad about that. Shouldn't poke fun at the innocent. Then again, what did he know about this man? He sat for a while in silence. Couldn't take it any longer and addressed the semi-absent man.

Mind if I call you Tom? Well, Tom, and Green gave a deep exhale, I don't know what to tell you. Truth is I don't know much. Truth is I'm no different from you. I don't have any answers. At this point though, maybe you're out of questions. I guess I can't know that. Tom? Can you hear me? Tom. Are you listening?

Green took another deep breath. Stared at the man in the bed.

You ever raise any children? There's this boy.

Hesitated, not sure how to continue. Then realized it didn't matter.

There's this boy. Gus Hawkins. He's come to stay with me for a while. I never had any kids of my own. Never married. Dated some, but that was some time ago. Spend most of my days alone. With my thoughts. Now I'm older. Not so old I guess. But old enough that those things I used to long for might not ever happen. I guess I still long for them. What did you do with your life's shortcomings, Tom? Or were you one of those people that never had any? Not sure they exist. I think some people are more malleable, able to take what comes and make lemonade out of rocks. I wasn't ever quite that way. I guess over time I just pushed it out of my mind, or, well, to the back of my mind. Focus on the now, on today. That's what I try to do. Sometimes I lay awake at night and that's when the things I haven't paid attention to begin to surface. I wonder, is this something I'll regret or feel like I missed out on when I get to the end of my life? The longing's still there. Never went away. Like an arthritis or something. Comes and goes. Flares up with the weather. What are your regrets, Tom?

The sound of the oxygen ticking and hissing. Dank smell of old man.

I guess my only hope for heaven or afterlife is that once we pass on, the longings and regret stay here in this world. Maybe they pass on too. I just hope we don't have to take them with us. That would be a terrible thing.

Green ruminated on that last thought for a while. Long enough that he lost track of time. Came to.

Where has the time gone, Tom? I guess I'd better move on. Let's say a prayer. You a Lord's Prayer kind of guy? You seem like a Lord's Prayer kind of guy.

Bowed his head. Uttered the words. Emptied mind. He opened his eyes and saw Deb's head poking through the door.

Ah, she said. Prayer. That's good. I heard voices and wondered who was talking to who in here. Thought that's some mighty powerful God stuff you got if you can get that one to talk.

Ah, yes. No. Prayer.

Green was embarrassed. Stood and accompanied her into the hallway.

Well, what'd you think of your first visit?

This is a wonderful place you have here.

Not too depressing? Winked at him.

No. I had a very nice conversation with that Twila.

She's a firecracker, isn't she?

That's a fact.

Deb laughed. I guess you got her pegged.

I wouldn't say that.

They made it to the lobby and he was heading for the door. The light of midday came through the windows, painting the room with brightness reflected off the snow outside.

I'm just kidding. Twila's a hoot. We have a good time here.

They stood in the lobby.

What else is on your agenda while you're down in the big city? she asked.

Oh, just a few errands I guess. Nothing too terribly exciting. Mostly just the grocery store.

Don't get too crazy, she said.

Green smiled. She was poking fun. Not too many people poked fun at him, he found. It endeared her to him that she treated him like an equal, not some being on a pedestal like some of the folks in his congregation. He must have been lingering because after a moment lost in thought, she said, I'd better let you get on with your day, but you come back anytime. This is about the most excitement we've had all week.

Oh, I don't know about that.

She nudged him, that playful, almost-flirting tease that she seemed prone to. Green wondered if she was this way with everyone. He thought that she was, yet he still allowed himself a bit of good feeling associated with the idea that there was something about him that brought out this behavior in her. Pushed that aside. *A little too self-centered*, he thought.

Well, I know Twila will be looking forward to next month.

Winked at him and Green could feel himself blush. *Leave it*, he thought.

I'd better get going, said Green.

Alright. I'll let you go. But don't be a stranger. You're one of us now.

Inside his head Green heard a droning chant: *One of us! One of us!* He smiled and said goodbye. Walked out into the cold sun and that flawless western sky, air so crisp it clove before him, and the drive home was filled with the daydreams of a younger man.

Tom

The drab cabin floor, gray and dusty, streaked with footprints. Tom lay across it, stared down the length of it. All day. Nothing to pass the time but the haunted corn maze of his own thoughts. Sunrise. Sunset. Cycle of the moon. Storms came and went. Lay on the floor and stared up, eyes seeing nothing. Somewhere in there his thoughts strayed into mutinous realms. In his right hand, a shell casing with the bullet still lodged in the nose of it. Tom spun it between his fingers. The cold brass. Heavy lead and the shift of the powder. Held the lead tip of the copper-cased bullet point to his temple and imagined pulling the trigger. Explosion. Propulsion. The lead mushroomed out when it hit bone. Tore its way through the frontal lobe. By then he'd know what it was like. He'd be done with before it ripped out the far side.

Death. The long darkness. Or something . . . else. Ruminated on that. His mother was already there. Gone on and he would not get back the times that he'd lost. Her death was a weight on him. His father's discerning gaze heavy on his mind, heavy as the hand he'd felt so many times throughout his upbringing. The guilt. He was busy, what he told himself. That would never be forgiven. His mother's cancer grew and his distance grew with it. Bad timing. If only it had come at a different time, though what would have been better? Nothing. He couldn't be happy. Blamed his father for this. His upbringing. It was endless. The voices in his mind carried the message. Uncontrolled interjection. Held him back.

The feeling of loneliness had come as a surprise to Tom. In his adult life he'd become such a solitary creature that he believed there was no level of isolation he could not withstand, but being cut off completely from the rest of mankind? Well, that was a different sort of loneliness. A part of him longed to hear the voice of another human. Another part of him hoped never to see another person as long as he lived. *Not true*, he thought. There was at least one person he still wanted to see. Gus. Where was he now? How was he faring? Tom had not yet lost all sense of rationality. The boy would in all likelihood hate him for being the cause of his father's death, even if the absence of the man could be seen as something of a relief. No more abuse to weather. Made Tom think of his own father. The things he'd suffered at Tom Sr.'s hands. The bruises left when he'd struck him as a boy. He didn't think he'd ever be able to let go of the hatred he had for his father, and yet, there was still a part of him that wanted to see that man just one more time. Lay eyes on him. Tell him . . . something. As if simple words could release the lifelong burden of resentment.

He walked to the shed to pass the time. Looked in on the moose quarters. Made sure nothing was gnawing there. Some mouse turds in the frozen pools of blood below the hanging meat. He carried in wood. Stocked up on kindling. Slept. He slept out of boredom, and upon waking the long hours stretched out before him.

He went outside when the sun hit the meadow. Took a pair of wood-framed snowshoes laced with straps of leather from the shed and set out across to the trees on the far side. The depths of winter though here and there, hints of inklings of the spring to come. Days growing longer. He measured them with an absent mind. Noted from time to time the early light of the day, the height of the sun in the sky. Warmth of an afternoon, drips of liquid water falling from the eaves. Beyond the meadow was a spring, and he'd packed in a solid path between there and the cabin. Filled what containers he could find and thus had fresh water to drink without the work of melting snow. Returned to the cabin and whiled away the long hours. Hours of thought and remembering, twisting the memories into something that slew him. Wondered if his father ever felt the weight of their history. Tom wasn't holding his breath on that. He'd never get back the things that were taken from him.

Gus

Gus stood along the fence at the edge of the playground. The cold of February had broken and March had brought warmer temperatures, almost springlike, though everyone in town knew better than to trust that winter was truly over. This day was overcast and warm, the snow on the asphalt turned to slush. A few other boys from his grade played nearby. Gus lingered on the outskirts. He watched them, almost interacting as part of the group but reluctant to immerse himself. Watched their movements, heard the things they said. The playful insults lobbed back and forth. They didn't include him in this part of their world and he was glad for that, not sure how to respond. What he desired most was approval, and he studied them, subconsciously figuring a way to win it.

Two girls shuffled their feet along the playground, meandering, talking. Kicked one of the few remaining chunks of ice through the piles of slush and dirty streams and puddles. They talked between themselves, low voices. Giggled at some shared joke. They came close to where the group of boys huddled, and Gus fidgeted against the chain link that delineated the border of the school property. If the girls had been paying more attention, had not been engrossed in their world, they might have steered clear of the group of boys, given them a wider berth. It was not their first encounter with these boys that were prone to harsh words. One of them, Gina, had been a regular target, and it came as no surprise when, as they walked past the group, one of the boys lunged out and barked at them, yelling as a follow-up, I'm sorry. I thought you were a dog. Returned to words of consent, jostles of approval from his peers.

Gus watched. He knew Gina, not well, yet perhaps better than he knew any other children. They had been neighbors for a time. Saw her take the other girl's hand and usher her away, a few hushed words discerned only by the two. They walked down the fence and continued their meandering lap of the playground.

The boys were still laughing at their jest, the one who'd said it standing taller and smiling wider than the others. Gus leaned on the fence. He smiled too, as if he were included. None of the boys paid him any mind. Kept an equal eye to the group and the other on the playground. The goings-on there of the other children. The playground and swing set awash in running and giggling and yelling. He watched Gina and her friend. They walked slow and kept to themselves. Acted as if the incident of the boys yelling at them had not happened at all. When they came closer again, the boys picked up little pieces of snow and tossed them at them, missing most of the time, though a few small slush balls splattered at their feet. Gus was still watching. Without thinking he had moved closer, near the group. He held in his hands a chunk of solid ice the size of his fist and he lobbed it at the girls, overwhelmed by the urge to participate. Gina's friend turned her head at the last second and the ice ball clocked her on the nose and blood erupted without warning across her lips and down onto her jacket.

The group of boys went silent and, heads bowed, dispersed, sensing the consequences to come and not wanting to be a part of them. The teacher on duty came over and tended to the girl's bloody nose and Gus watched as her arm raised and her finger pointed at him. He looked around and he was alone, standing by the fence along the edge of the playground.

Green was at home when he got the call. Had been getting ready to head down to Bonfisk and run a few errands, do his rounds at the home. Was cleaning the few dishes left from breakfast when the phone rang.

He found Gus in the counselor's office, back slumped in a wooden chair.

Come in, Morris, said Cathy.

Green stepped into the room and sat in a second

wooden chair beside Gus. He didn't say anything at first and neither did anyone else so the three of them sat there in silence. Cathy broke the stalemate.

Thanks for coming in, Morris.

Green nodded. Looked at Gus, who stared at the edge of the desk before him.

We all know what happened. I don't think we need to go into detail. Gus. She paused and waited. Gus, she said again.

Gus looked up. Made eye contact. Glanced at Green.

Why did you throw the ice ball?

After a moment Gus shrugged. Said nothing.

Cathy took a deep breath. Green was quiet. He felt sorry for the boy. Sorry for the girl with the busted nose, but he couldn't bring himself to blame Gus for acting out. Seeking attention? That didn't seem to be Gus's way, but then again, attention from whom? Kids can have a funny way of attempting to garner one another's affection. Green thought of the other girl. The group of boys. The social pressures of being a child.

There has to be some kind of repercussion, said Cathy.

Green nodded. Cathy looked to Gus.

I'm sending you home today, and I think one day of out-of-school suspension is within order. That's the lower end of the spectrum, mind you.

Her face and tone of voice held a margin of apology in them. She turned back to Green.

And he'll be marked as a zero for any missed assignments today or tomorrow.

It was not clear how much the boy was registering, though Green thought it likely Gus was taking in every word.

This is going to set you farther back in your schoolwork. Cathy looked at Gus as she spoke, but Green felt a pang of guilt, as if this had all been his fault. He was responsible for helping Gus maintain a passing grade, keeping him up on his assignments. If the boy fell too far behind, well, Green hoped it would not come to that, but Gus did not seem to be doing himself any favors. If it happens again, Cathy went on, the punishment will be more severe.

Of course, said Green. Then he added, We'll have a talk.

It was not clear if Green was saying this to Gus as a means to warn him or if it was for the counselor's benefit, to show that he was up for the challenge of disciplining the boy. Green himself was not sure for whose benefit he had said it. This whole encounter made him uncomfortable, not the very least because the boy, still, in his mind, could do no wrong. It was the world and life, after all, that had harmed the boy, and in many ways it could be argued that any anger Gus had was justified, even if the outlet of that anger remained objectionable.

The odd pair walked out through the empty hallways and into the parking lot. Gus dragged his feet, gaze downcast. Green, sensing a vulnerable moment, said nothing.

Allowed the boy the solitude of his thoughts. The remainder of the day, little was said between them. Gus read his book and then watched TV in the evening. Green penciled notes on the upcoming sermon. When it was the boy's bedtime, an arbitrary 8:00 p.m. that Green had determined to be appropriate, Green turned the television off and sent the boy up to brush his teeth. Did the perfunctory "tuck-in," foregoing any physical affection that an actual parent might express, no kiss good night, and sent himself to bed, where he lay awake long into the night.

PART II

Tom

Spring broke along the high country in fits and starts. The sun began to hold and melted the surface of the snow in the afternoons, freezing at night to create a supportive crust. Then a storm would come in and turn the world to winter again for a few days. Tom had lost track of the passage of time and it was hard for him to tell the date. Could have been early March of a warm year or even early April after a harsh winter. Tom figured somewhere in late March to be a solid bet as the winter had been a decent one with good snow and some bitter cold snaps but nothing extraordinary.

In this time, a warm spell drew Tom from the cabin. A few birds had come in and taken up residence around the edge of the woods. He wondered what they fed on this early in the year. Perhaps dead insects or seeds revealed by melting snow. He wasn't sure. Tom had never been a bird person. Some birds spent all winter in the mountains, and he figured it was early enough that most of the ones he saw were of this variety, though with the shift in the weather it seemed plausible that a few early migrators could have come up to this elevation.

At any rate, the warmer days gave Tom a new lease on life. As the days grew longer, he spent more time outside. He hadn't been wearing sufficient clothing when he fled into the mountains to allow him comfort in the winter temperatures, but the early part of spring was different. His ratty jeans and long underwear, threadbare and filthy, were enough as the days warmed by late morning to allow for more outside time. The sun on his face was pleasant and drove out the desperation he'd settled into when the days were shorter. The moose meat provided ample calories, though he still felt the lack of a diverse diet and tired easily. Craved fruit like nothing he'd ever felt before.

As Tom rekindled a will to live, he began to think on what he might do next. Remote enough and not widely known, the cabin had sufficed to hide him through the winter, but he knew it could not last. It made sense to him that no one had come knocking while the hills were bound in snow, but the summer would allow for easier access and he couldn't be sure that no one would investigate eventually. And the food. He always came back to food. Tom had always been a skilled woodsman, able to thrive in the wilderness, but he could not last indefinitely. As he pondered, there was really only one viable option he could see. The Horak family ranch. He could get there. Knew the way like he knew himself. Or used to know himself. Things had gone haywire and he no longer felt like the man he'd been. But the way was there. The familiar hills and woods and clearings. Could call them to mind, clear as photographs.

On an impulse he made a decision. It happened that quick. He spent a day preparing. Didn't take long, really. Not much there. Most of the work was in the meat, what was left of it, a fair bit. The days had warmed enough that the meat had thawed. He cut it from the bone and piled it into plastic trash bags and strapped them to a frame pack he'd found in the shed along with an axe that he thought he might use if he needed to make wood for a fire. That evening he built a roaring blaze in the woodstove and sat cross-legged with his eyes closed, sweating. Fell asleep and woke before sunrise, long before or just before, he couldn't say. A full moon lit up the night, the world illuminated by the glow of snow on the ground. He dressed. Did not bother to stoke the stove or even latch the cabin door as he stepped outside and strapped the snowshoes to his feet. Shouldered the pack and rifle. The sun-affected surface of the snow was hard and supported his weight, crunched beneath the wooden frames of the snowshoes. He paused midway across the meadow and looked about.

This was silence. Complete stillness. He closed his eyes and listened, envisioned the way forward, the way he knew but had not seen in a number of years. With a breath of not frigid-winter but only cold-spring air, he walked.

TOM HORAK WAS BORN ON A FULL MOON IN LATE winter, the bright moon huge in the sky like some vibrant and shiny bauble tinted the slightest of reds. He was one of three babies born that night in that little hospital in the arid sage country on the edge of the mountains. The night staff there said that constituted a landslide in a county where you might get a baby a week, maybe only a few a month, if that. It was the moon, they said. Tom's mother knew it was the moon. Said she could feel it coming days ahead of time. She knew the moon was coming, that was easy enough, just look at the calendar on the wall above the kitchen table. But the baby. That was something else. Something inside her, deep in the connective tissue of her body, a subtle energy. Call it intuition, she told her husband when he asked how she knew. She could tell he didn't buy it. He wouldn't say it outright. That wasn't his way. He would not have wanted to hurt her feelings in what he felt was her delicate state, though he was far from anything resembling a sensitive man, not even a good man in the eyes of many, and just a sideways glance at his facial expression could tell his wife things going on in his head that even he was unaware of.

It was a straightforward birth, absent of complications, and they drove home the following morning with the sun blaring down out of a clear western sky. The patched asphalt wound through the Pronged Hills outside of town; then the paved road ended and there was a decent long way to go over the gravel in the bed of a narrow valley before they came to the ranch where the father had lived for damn near all his life. He'd met his wife through some family friends. She'd come up in Delta County to the west, the daughter of the children of homesteaders, some of the last to homestead on that land in a time when such a thing could be done. Those days were dead and gone, long gone, by the time the two were wed and settled in the ranch that his parents had bought for a pittance off some gigantic holding parceled off by the family that had owned it for generations, the folks who'd claimed it as their own in the times when white folk were drawing lines on maps of ground they'd never laid eyes on. The original inhabitants, the Utes, were no longer there, not in any measurable way. The ones that weren't killed off or starved or poisoned or that hadn't fallen ill had been forcibly removed. It was said that the spirits of those that had died through the course of eons still roamed the hills and woods, though most never witnessed them, or didn't notice.

Tom Horak the senior was white as could be, in both a physical and cultural sense of the meaning. Some German and Irish on one side from a farming family that went back a number of generations, their history and westward migration paralleling that of the great expansion of the federal state. The other side was descended from Slovak and Croatian immigrants brought to the area to take up the less savory tasks in the many coal mines that were in operation there from around the mid-nineteenth to the mid-twentieth centuries.

The ranch itself was a good piece of ground with a long sloping pasture in the valley bottom crossed with ditches that were fed by a decent stream that ran year-round. The gravel road snaked alongside the pasture at the base of a dry hill peppered with rocks and sagebrush and a spindly grass that stayed green for a just a few ephemeral weeks in early summer. In the ranch yard, the yard, as Tom Sr. called it, there was an old barn and a house, both original structures built there in the late 1800s. Of course the house had been added on to, the roof and windows replaced at some point in Tom Sr.'s childhood. A few outbuildings held livestock and farm implements. Chickens wandered about and a tractor was parked by the entrance to the barn with its bucket turned down so it would not catch the rain.

•

As Tom Jr., or Tommy, as his father would have called him, crouched in a group of spindly aspens on the hillside overlooking the ranch, there was none of that, or none of the activity. The barn was still standing, its wide sliding door ajar. The house, his childhood home, was there. Still looked the same, perhaps some fading color from years of sunlight beating down. Certainly the tin on the roof had faded, red to rust to bare metal in places, scraped by the snows of more than a half century of winters. A run-down tractor. Fuel tanks. The old dump in a hollowed-out patch of hillside. A graveyard of rusted-out old vehicles. Snow still covered much of the ground with only a few patches of dirt or rock poking through. Beyond the buildings the line of the road, unplowed, wound down along the pasture. He surveyed the property through the scope of the rifle. Watched for a long time until he was satisfied that no one was about the place.

When he rose to walk down the hillside with matted hair and a scrappy beard plastered uneven on his face, gums bleeding from scurvy, he must have been terrifying to behold. A mountain man drawn from another time. He thought of the load of raw meat on his back and wondered if he were to come across another human, what would they make of him? Hell, he wasn't sure he knew what to make of himself. Somewhere over the course of the last couple months he'd lost track of that.

The going had been rough. His quads burned like fire from the weight of the pack. Shoulders tight and his neck cramped, pain like a knife. At this lower elevation, the seasons had progressed further into true spring than they had at the cabin in the mountains. As he descended farther, the snowshoes became cumbersome with rocks and foliage poking up through the snow, so he stopped to remove them. Had to take the meat-heavy pack off to reach a kneeling position, and he slung the snowshoes over the axe handle on the side of the pack. As he began to walk again he post-holed through the crusted snow to the top of his shins. When he reached the flats the crust was thick enough that it supported him in places, making for a broken jerky walk as he made a few clean steps then broke through without warning. At last he came into the yard that sat atop a subtle hill and the snow thinned and hardened. Went first to the barn. Stood in the big bay door. A few ancient hay bales, the twine rotted through, accordioned out and half submerged in the chaff of countless seasons. Where the pile of dusty hay tapered off to bare ground, a cast-iron tub with claw feet, one of them missing, sat improbably in the center of the room. A remnant of the hordes of objects collected over the course of his father's life, a few of the objects from before even his time. On the back wall, a stack of mongrel scraps of sheet metal and pallets. The odd rusted tractor implement outdated by a couple generations of innovation. The storage room in the corner by the large front door.

He turned and walked up to the house. The yard seemed bare to him. He'd helped clean it up when his father moved out ten years ago, so its sparseness should not have come as a surprise, yet without the objects for reference, the sounds of animals, life and abundance emanating from all directions, it seemed like another place altogether, or that place in a different time, one in which he was a stranger . . .

●

AND YET, THERE HE IS AS A BOY STANDING ON THE buck-and-rail fence of a corral in the very early morning, his breath rising in gasps of steam that hover and dissipate while his father on horseback repeats, Heeyaw, heeyaw, and grunts beside a small group of heifers and their calves. The smell of mud and animals and shit and the scrape of a canvas collar turned up against his neck. The wind rises, whistles off the peak of the barn roof. Tom doesn't mind the work or the early mornings or even the cold. One of the few places his father treats him like something resembling an equal, long as he doesn't screw anything up. Then there'd be hell to pay, but not this day.

He watches his father work the cattle. He separates a calf and gets it over by the gate and Tom jumps down and swings it open so his father can push it through where it stands on the frozen ground of the next pen over bawling for its mother. His own mother is up at the house. There'll be a hot breakfast on the table when they finish and get back up. That is the expectation, and so it is. Then his mom will drive him down the road to catch the bus to school. He stares out at the hills and thinks about nothing, about the sleep he wishes he was still having. Thinks about school and how tired he will be. The chores he'll have to do when he gets home. The brightness of emerging sunlight on the snow makes him squint.

●

Tom shielded his eyes to the midday sun and walked on up to the house. The front door was locked and he walked around to the side door that let into the kitchen. The knob turned but he had to throw his shoulder against it to pop the door from its frame and it swung inward, hinges rasping with a light coating of rust. He set his pack and rifle up against the cabinets that half circled the room, with the sink on the wall below the window there. The space on the end where a refrigerator once stood. The round table was still there in the center of the kitchen. Film of dust like a thick mold grown up on every surface. He set the rifle on the table, trailed a finger along the back of one of the chairs and looked at the black grime that came up on his skin. Wiped it on his pant leg. Much of the furniture remained. The longer dining room table and uncomfortable chairs were visible through the vacant doorway.

He stood in that little room where the east-facing front door and the big windows took in the early light of mornings. Walked past the seldom-used dining room and into the living room. The rug was gone. Only a square of darker wood where it had lain for so many years. Also the sofa and reclining chair. Empty space and four black rust spots where the woodstove had been. He looked up. A bit of cloth wadded in the stub of chimney left in the ceiling. The stairs leading up from the corner on the back of the house were lit by a small window below the second story. Three rooms upstairs. The larger on the north side, that was his parents'. His room above the kitchen, and the smaller one in between that had been the study where his father kept his books and tied flies for fishing in the early days of Tom's childhood, good days, before his father turned.

The dark floors creaked as he walked along the railing in the hallway, and every room was empty. Dead flies speckled the ground, crossed shadows of the windowpanes where not even dust held in the light, all of it settled so long ago, though the memories remained. Raw as they'd ever been.

In the kitchen he rummaged in all the cabinets, coming up with a can of black beans, two of peas, and a fourth can without a label that was so bloated by pressure that he moved on without touching it. He pulled up a latch on the floor of the short hallway beside the bathroom. Descended a creaky wooden stairway. Hunching to walk, he struck a match and held it before him in the stale air. There were shelves built on the north wall. A lone half-gallon jar of canned peaches gleamed back at him, a beacon of gold in the otherwise drab cellar. He took it.

It was all but dark when he walked back through the snow and down to the barn. There among the scraps of refuse he found a square of tin and hauled it back up to the house. On subsequent trips he brought grayed and half-rotten pallets and a bundle of dry hay. He lit a fire on the tin in the living room. Got on a chair and pulled the cloth from the old stovepipe sticking out of the ceiling when the room filled with smoke. Ate a dinner of half a peach and a hunk of unsalted meat roasted over the flames on a stick pulled from the willows along the defunct irrigation ditch. The peaches were so sweet and delicate he ate three more halves for dessert and gulped down nearly half of the thick syrup they marinated in. Later, he fell asleep. Woke in frigid cold. Shoulder stiff and his arm was numb from sleeping on the bare floor. A fierce rumbling in his gut. Recalled the peaches. First fruit he'd eaten in months. He ran outside, tripped down the steps while undoing his pants, and fell with a wet bit of warmth running down the inside of his leg.

He'd been there for three days when he thought about ghosts. Not so much ghosts of the dead but rather ghosts of the past, if memories could come back as ghosts. The ghost of the child that he was. His father as a younger man. Though he supposed that his mother could be a ghost, dead as she was. Died over a decade past when Tom was in his early thirties, cut down by a sneaking form of cancer, not so much sneaking as it was ignored. Tom blamed his father for this, his mother ever saintlike in his mind. Tried not to think about it. Brought up certain of his own shortcomings. The time he'd spent with her. The things his father said. Guilt and shame like a disease, festering in his bones. Tom didn't see or hear his mother in the house or anywhere about the place. What he heard and perhaps saw inside his mind were things from his early years that he had not thought of in a long time and that had been dormant for long enough that they had been forgotten, entrenched in his psyche. Then the things he saw were no longer in his mind. He wandered the house and replayed the memories as they came to him and wondered if that was exactly the way it had been.

•

HE IS AT THE TABLE WITH HIS FATHER TO HIS LEFT
at the head, his mother across from him, the wall at her
back adorned by a watercolor still life of a bouquet of
purple lupine in a glass vase. Hanging lamp above them.
Dim light from the kitchen cuts across his father's back.
The tapping of cutlery on ceramic plates. His father stops,
forearms on the edge of the table. Turns from his mother
to him and back to his mother. Shakes his head. The boy
looks from his mother to his father. Back to his mother.
Searches for some cue about how he should act, some
semblance of a bearing. His mother's eyes are fixed on the
meal before her. His father. Sneering laughter. Mumbles
curse words under his breath.

His father has had his evening cocktails. Whiskey on
ice. Can't say how many, but a few. Definitely a few. That
is the norm. Tom has seen the transformation countless
times before. Not that his father is all that caring to begin
with, but after a few drinks he turns into a different man.
Cutting and cold. Malicious. Petty and sometimes violent.
He knows that this is not the time to speak up. It is a time
when it is best not to be seen. Not to be noticed. He keeps
his head down. Bracing for impact. At last his father can
take it no longer.

Jesus, he says. A morgue would be livelier than you two.

His father stands and takes his plate into the kitchen. Drops it hard in the sink and Tom hears the plate shatter. His father leaves the house. When he is gone his mother extends a hand toward her son, taps her fork on the edge of his plate. Says, Eat up. Your food's gettin cold.

Tom stares at his plate. Knows that to acknowledge would be to give in. An acceptance, of a kind. He must resist. Feels the energy burn inside him. Lets it run its course until it smolders. A light ache in his gut. As he eats slow, timid bites, his mother stands and goes to the kitchen. Picks up the shards of broken plate. Tom finishes his meal, the food turned to ashes on his tongue.

•

Tom walked back to the top of the stairs. Paced the hallway until he stopped in the doorway to his old bedroom and stood there, looking in.

He saw himself there on the bed sitting with his back to the door. The raised voice of his father came through the wall.

●

GODDAMNIT, BETHANY. YOU COULD RUIN A FUCKIN wet dream.

Hears the footsteps in the hallway and his father pauses outside his bedroom door. Looks in at his son. What the fuck are you cryin about?

His father stares. What are you, deaf? He says.

Tom says nothing. He hears his father's footsteps. Slow. Methodical. The man approaches. Towers over his son. Tom feels the touch of his father's fingers on his chin. Gentle and firm. The hard calloused skin raises the boy's face until they are eye to eye. Tom's cheeks are wet with tears. In a quiet, demanding voice, What are you cryin for?

Waits for the answer that will not come.

Girls cry. Are you a little girl? I thought you were a big boy. Didn't you say that?

Then the strike. Tom feels a hard, sharp pain on the left side of his face. It was not a full swing, a taunting open-handed slap, almost lazy, but the pain is there, the small boy's head knocked off-kilter. A brief pause and then his father strikes him once more.

Tom cannot speak. His chin puckers and lips tremble. His father's fingers are on his chin again. The touch hardens. He feels the hand tremble. Sees the face tighten. He braces himself.

Tom closes his eyes and waits. The touch from his father's hand grows harder until with a firm push the boy's neck kicks back and he hears the footsteps moving away from him. Down the stairs and out of the house. The silence that remains is blaring and pulsates with a sickening rhythm.

Tom stares at the patch of rug between his legs, hands resting on his thighs, shallow breath. Raises a fist and brings it down hard on the soft meat above his knee. Again, in the same spot, until the pain goes numb. In the morning, there is a green-yellow bruise and it hurts when he walks.

●

All in a moment he recalled the only time he'd stood up to his father. He could not remember how it began, only that tempers flared, voices were raised. He had looked up past his oppressor's chin and said with all the anger of his childhood . . .

•

I HATE YOU.

The shocked look on the man's face turns to outrage at the occurrence of something he'd created rebelling so definitively against him. Tom turns his back and goes upstairs to his room. Slams the door shut and locks it.

Footsteps rattle on the stairs and the wood of the door cracks against the frame.

Open the goddamn door.

The banging continues until the door swings open and Tom slips past. Feels his father's hands reach for him, fingers catching on the fabric of his clothes for only a moment and then he is free. Down the stairs and out into the night. Cries of, You get back here, fade behind him. Light from the porch disappears when he rounds the bend in the road and slows to a walk.

Cool, dry air. The soft noise his stocking feet make in the loose gravel. Then the bouncing illumination of a flashlight and he bolts up the embankment to the main ditch overhung by willows. Feet slip soundless into the cold water. Perched on the far bank with his legs submerged to the knee. Crouching, moisture from the damp bank seeps through the seat of his pants. Shallow breath on the smooth surface of slow-flowing irrigation. Seething, he watches as the light comes down the drive and passes. Teeth clenched as his father shouts.

Get back here, boy.

Then, Tommy.

Again, Tommy.

After a while he hears footsteps on the road, the flash-light extinguished. Then a door slams shut.

He climbs from the ditch on the uphill side. Cuts above the barn, stopping to take a box of matches from a shelf in the supply room. In the draw where they shoot rifles, a fire ring and stack of split aspen where they used to come as a family and spend an afternoon on the weekends in sum-mer, fire kindling as the light drew thin, burning down to embers. The quiet walk home in the dark. As steam rises from his socks draped over a stone, he tries to think of the last time they'd done anything like that as a family. It was a long time ago. The good memories buried beneath phrases his father threw about like stones, the ubiquity of them rendering every slander meaningless.

They'd been shooting. Target practice. The boy was a crack shot. No rise or fall of the gunsight with his breath. Just deadlocked. But that day everything had gone to hell. His mother and father were bickering. His father's slow pulls from the flask. What the hell is wrong with you? A repeated question thrown at his son every time his shot went awry.

The targets were tin cans perched on a log at the back of the camp where a grove of aspens spanned a low rise along the hill. Beyond that the shoulder of a mountain was vis-ible on the horizon. As Tom lay on the ground in a prone position, the length of the barrel stuck out before him, his eyes wandered to the mountain shoulder. Leaves in the woods bristled in a faint breeze. He heard the sound they made, tinkling off one another like falling paper shards. Smelled the humus of decomposing soil. Felt the press of the ground on his body. A root nested into the bottom of his ribs. The senses drowned out the voice of his father, his mother's soft acquiescence and placations. Distracted him from the mundane task of pulling the trigger. His father focused solely on the mistakes. Every missed shot fell like a personal insult. His father said everything and nothing under spirit-laden breath, blurring into the eternity of every day of his childhood.

After shooting for a bit, his mother called him for lunch. His father took a round on the .22 while mother and son sat on folding latticed lawn chairs next to a cold firepit lined with head-sized stones and ate sandwiches and potato chips and sliced apples. The woman watched her son. Saw the slumped shoulders, a bend in his upper back.

Tom, she said. Only his mother ever called him Tom. To nearly everyone else he was Tommy. He looked at her. Do you remember the time we went over to Memaw and Papaws, just the two of us? He squinted up at her, a half-eaten piece of apple in one hand. You were pretty young, she went on, but I bet you can remember. We stayed for a whole week in the peak of apple season. While your dad was off on a bowhuntin trip? You remember?

He watched his mother reach up a hand and wipe a finger along the bottom length of an eye, and it came away wet, glistening in the afternoon light. He stared at her, not sure what this meant. Relaxed when she smiled.

We were out pickin in the orchard and I tossed a little one toward you and it hit you square between the eyes and bounced directly into your tote. We laughed so hard I thought one of us was gonna wet themselves for sure. Later you ate too many apples and gave yourself the runs.

She smiled and another tear appeared in the corner of her eye. Got it with a motion that looked like she was scratching an itch. Do you remember that? she asked.

Tom had stopped eating. He looked at his mother, not smiling, lost in concentration. I think so, he said. He could not remember and wanted his mother to believe that he did. Could not tell if he had succeeded in this.

His mother reached out a hand and patted him on the knee. His father returned and sat near them. Can I get one a them sandwiches?

His mother's touch and gaze lingered. Then she pulled away and tended to his father. That was the last and only time Tom and his mother talked of the day in the apple orchard. He sat there while his mother focused on the man. It was one or the other. Never room for both at the same time. He thought she did it to shield him from his father, placate the monster that slumbered beneath the surface of the man's skin. After a time, Tom stopped paying attention to the adults. Watched the ants that crawled here and there, picking up tidbits of fallen food to carry back to their nest. Could smell the air, the woods. That smell that would stick with him for the rest of his life and brought up memories of this time with his family. The good times peppered throughout the nonsense of his childhood. The sadness. The anger. The simmering defeat.

As Tom sits by the fire remembering that afternoon, more than the actual memory of it, he remembers the underlying tension of the day. It comes as a feeling in his body, pressure building, and at any moment he could burst. He hears the tiny murmurings of discord that surfaced as they had eaten sandwiches around the cold fire ring. As if without speaking they'd all decided to force themselves through the motions of things no longer felt in the heart.

Later in life he would think of that time long ago, wishing with pangs of regret that he'd stood up to the man more than he did, maybe hit him, because at least through violence there could be release.

He does not sleep that night. When he walks through the kitchen door in the predawn gloom, his mother sits at the table with coffee and the radio playing, mending a button on one of his father's shirts. Without looking up, she says, He's down in the barn. You need to go apologize.

Smoldering resentment toward her he does not acknowledge or understand. His father is the one who ought to be apologizing, though he never would. Never understanding the sting of words. The lasting, unseen scars when the bruises faded. Deep wounds that would only fester.

He heads down to the barn. Finds his father in the corner fiddling with a piece of rusted machinery. Tom Sr. looks up, the anger gone and in its place a kind of sorrow. He rises to his feet and waits for the boy to speak.

I'm sorry.

Do really hate me?

No.

Good. Cause I love you.

I love you too.

His father takes him in a firm embrace only half returned, the boy's anger masked, turned inward, wishing he had the courage to tell the man how he really feels. That it is true. He really does hate him.

●

The next one came unbidden. Tom didn't recall this memory often, though it came to him in moments of intense despair and anger. Always he felt rage pulsing in his body afterward, as if a poison seed were planted there, shoved in without consent, by the hands of his father.

•

TOM IS TWELVE YEARS OLD, THE SAME AGE GUS IS
when his father is taken from him. He is on his knees in
the center of the barn. Can hear the slow scuff of boots as
his father walks around him.

I'm goin to have to teach you, the man says. If you can't
learn on your own the things you should know without
havin to be taught, then I will teach you.

Hears the belt buckle unclasp, the leather slithering
through belt loops.

It was a simple thing, a thing that any child would do.
Tom did not see the wrong in it, certainly not when he'd
done it, and he doesn't see it now as his father prepares the
punishment. The best he can manage is that his father is
angry and anything that angers the man is wrong.

A man had come to the ranch that morning to pick up
a load of hay bales. Tom recognized the man, he'd come
before, but he did not know him well. When the man arrived, Tom, his father, and the man walked down to the
barn to look at the hay. His father talked of quality, the
season they'd had and how the grass had grown. The man
looked, ran his fingers over the top of a bail, pulled some
chaff in his fingers and lifted it to his nose to smell it. Satisfied, he looked at Tom. Go on and fetch my truck, he said.
Tossed Tom a set of keys. Smiled as he did it. Though Tom
was only twelve, he'd learned to drive at ten and had been

driving a stick shift for six months. Ranch kids grew up young, a necessity of the life they lived.

Tom held the keys in his hand and jogged across the yard. He got in the truck, started it, and began to pull around. As he did, he saw something shiny in the cup holder, a pile of loose change. Without a second thought, he grasped a quick handful, a few coins, some larger than others, and stuffed them in his pocket. Parked the truck before the sliding barn doors and hopped out to help load the hay. While they worked, he felt the weight of the coins in his pocket, heard them jingle when he moved quick or climbed in or out of the truck bed. They arranged the bails like a loose puzzle. Secured them with ratchet straps, and the man handed Tom Sr. a folded wad of cash that neither counted. Took another single bill and handed it to the kid. Thanked him for his help.

When the man left, Tom went up to the house. In his room, the door half open, he emptied the change onto his bed with the five-dollar bill the man had given him. He counted. One dollar and sixty-seven cents plus the five. As he admired the coins and bill, he did not hear his father slip into the room but felt the presence of the man standing over him. Looked up to a blank stare that looked back, unwavering.

Where'd you get that?

Tom said nothing, his mouth falling open. He knew that to speak would be catastrophic. There was nothing he could say that would make things go better for him. He knew that his father knew the money was not his. Tom Sr. kept close tabs on these sorts of things, one of the many aspects of Tom's life left firmly in the senior's control. He had no allowance, no other way to make money.

Where'd you get that from?

Tom was still speechless. A crack to the side of the head loosened his tongue.

I found it, he said.

Found it? Where'd you find it?

No response. Another crack on the head.

In the cup holder. When I moved the truck. It was in the cup holder.

Tom was crying now. Words struggled out through whimpering tears.

His father said nothing. Scooped up the change along with the five-dollar bill and stuffed them into his pocket. Then he grabbed Tom by the scruff of his shirt neck and led him through the house. His mother in the kitchen.

What's goin on?

Tom Sr. shot her a look. Said, Stay out of this, Bethany.

Then they were out of the house. Tom being half led, half drug across the yard and into the barn.

So Tom kneels as his father holds the folded belt in his hands.

Take off your shirt, his father says, and Tom obeys.

His body is scrawny. A lean boy, always has been. The

air in the barn is cool and his skin puckers, perhaps as much from fear as temperature.

His father's footsteps stop. Tom hears him breathe. A pause and the belt strikes the child's back. Again. Pause. Again.

At first Tom counts the strikes. One. Two. Three. The fourth strike breaks him and the only thing he can register is searing pain. He collapses forward.

Get up, says his father.

Tom pushes halfway into a kneeling position when the belt strikes him again.

His father's breathing. Says, You always have to learn the hard way, don't you?

Tom never saw the fistful of loose change again, nor the five-dollar bill he'd earned stacking hay.

•

The memory faded. Tom felt the strops on his back then, the slicing slap of the leather. Slammed his palm on the doorjamb, cried out, and felt his wrist jam. Whenever this memory was recalled, he inevitably caused himself some sort of pain. Broke something. The rage bursting out of him without control.

Tom stood in the doorway to his old bedroom, heart thumping in his throat. Walked down the stairs with the energy ebbing out through shaky steps. Got a fire going on the piece of tin on the floor. Sat huddled beneath a blanket, the edge of it pulled up over his head like a hood. Rocked to the heat, beating thrum of memory after memory. He thought a lot about his father. Knew that he was still living, or that he was last he'd heard, which was some months ago now, yet he sensed that was still the case. He thought a little bit of his mother. About how he wished he had known her better. Of course he knew her, in every way that a child can know its loving mother, but as an adult he could not say that he really knew her. He knew things about her. That she liked to sew. Read from the Bible every day. Loved his father and loved her son more. But he couldn't rightly say that he knew either of his parents well as adults. That transition from childhood to adulthood, the transformation of those relationships, had not taken place, not in the way that he thought they had for other folks. In many ways Tom had gotten stuck in the past, his mind lingering on certain feelings, resentments, the times he'd been let down. Or worse. The disconnect of things that happened and never got resolved, bitterness clutched to like warmth in the cold. It was cold again. He'd let the fire burn out. He kindled another then lay down and fell asleep.

Marshal Tomlinson

*T*hinkin on this damn Hawkins situation is enough to drive me up a wall. Gets me thinkin about my boys. What I woulda done if I was in one situation or the other. Someone come to harm one a my children, I don't know what I woulda done. I was a practicin lawman when they was young. Can't say as that woulda kept things civil. There's few things in life that will drive any man to violence. Push them over the brink. I've never been there, though Lord knows they've been difficult times.

I got a good relationship with my sons. We've had our differences. Specially my firstborn. It can be hard to be the oldest son. I don't know why that is but it is. The youngest was a bit of a hellion but he was the baby. Got away with a lot. His older brother was straightlaced from the get-go. Put a lot of pressure on himself. I probly put a lot of pressure on him too. We come to work things out after he was grown. We had our moments though.

Sometimes I used to go for drives when things would get tough. Long aimless endeavors along county roads through the dark hours of the day. Time to clear my head and set things straight with myself on what's really important. I find myself doin that now. Tryin to make sense a things. Wonderin how that boy will make it through life on the hand he's been dealt. Nothin is straightforward, even in the best of times. The road curves ever round the bend.

Green

Before Gus's arrival into Morris Green's life, the pastor had not appreciated how easy it should have been to plan his days. No one's needs to consider but his own. Now that he had the child with him, he had to remind himself to think of Gus in any plans that he made. The one-day suspension from school complicated the situation further because it fell on the day Green was scheduled to visit the Home, or rather, the day after. He'd postponed when he got the call from the school about the incident. The boy was too old for day care, though Green wasn't even sure how that worked. Did you just show up with a kid and they take him for the day? Where was day care anyway? Left with a lack of solutions, he decided it would be easiest if Gus tagged along. He figured Gus would be bored, but then again, this suspension was supposed to be a punishment.

They ate breakfast and made the drive with a few flakes of snow from a weak spring storm spitting from the sky, melting as they hit the asphalt and windshield. These late-March storms could pack a punch, but the results never lasted. When the sun came out, the inevitable spring would reign, though this close to the mountains the snow in the hay meadows along the highway was still deep, only the topmost of four wires on the fences exposed to the elements. It had been a good winter.

They didn't talk on the drive. Gus was prone to long bouts of silence, whether some coping mechanism or introspection, Green could not be sure, but he felt that to force conversation was not the best approach. He wasn't much of a talker himself, so the situation kind of worked. When they arrived, they both exited the vehicle without a word, each with a book tucked under his arm, Green with his Bible and Gus some graphic novel that he was reading. Gus had only brought the book after Green suggested he might want something to fill the time with.

The foyer was empty and quiet. The tinkle of the little bell as the front door swung open and closed announced their presence, and soon footsteps tacked out of the hollow hallway beyond the desk. Deb stepped into the room. Face lit up when she saw the boy.

You brought a friend, she said. I didn't know you had any friends.

Well, yes. This is Gus, said Green. He's, uh, out from school today.

I'm just kidding with ya, she said. Then to the boy, Whatcha got there?

Gus looked at the book tucked under his arm. A book, he said.

A book? Well, I can see that.

I thought maybe he could post up somewhere while I do the rounds, said Green.

Oh we can do better than that, said Deb. You want something to drink, Gus? Maybe some hot cocoa?

Gus did not say anything but Green could sense him lightening, easing into the situation.

Why don't you just come with me. She held out her hand.

Gus looked at the hand, at Green, then walked toward the woman. She seemed to sense that he would not take the offered hand, so turned and allowed the boy to follow her into the hallway from whence she'd come.

Green found Twila in her room. The few others. He sat with the old man on the oxygen tank. Listened to the *tick-hiss, tick-hiss* that was his world. Closed his eyes and sat in the dark space of his mind. When he'd finished, he went out to the lobby. Deb was sitting at the desk eating a sandwich.

How'd it go?

Oh, same old same old, said Green. Then, catching himself in a moment of unintended complaint, added, It was good.

The front door opened, the bell tinkling, and a man in the same uniform as Deb came in.

Hey, Doren, said Deb.

What's up, Deb, said Doren.

My replacement, she said to Green.

Ah, said Green. And all this time I thought you were the entirety of the operation.

I'm just the hired help, she said.

Yeah right, said Doren, emerging from the office with a set of keys. This place would fall apart without you.

Well, we all do our part.

Anything out of the ordinary? asked Doren.

I don't think so.

Deb disappeared into the office. Doren looked at Green, who suddenly felt like he was intruding. Looked to his side and there was Gus. It was the first time in a while that he had forgotten about the boy. How was the hot cocoa? he said.

Gus shrugged. Good, he said.

Good, said Green. Should we get going?

Deb reappeared from the office. I'll walk out with you, she said.

She led the way, with Green and Gus trailing behind her through the swinging glass doors.

What a beautiful day, said Deb.

The storm had cleared, the clouds burnt off, and though it was still fairly windy, there was a bit of sun that held some warmth to it when they were out of the full blast of the wind.

What are you two up to now?

I don't know, said Green. He looked at Gus, who gave no ideas of his own. Probably head back home here soon.

How about a walk? Deb suggested. I'll buy you a cup of coffee. We could go to the park. She cocked her head toward Gus.

What do you think, buddy? Green asked Gus, who gave his usual nonanswer, but Green thought he saw a note of excitement in the boy's eyes. Sure, he said. Why not.

The three of them left the home and walked the quiet streets. The sky held that blue that seemed almost not real, clouds trailing out of the west so high and thin it was hard to tell where sky ended and clouds began. The day was breezy, as springtime always was on the edge of the mountains. Green and Deb walked beside each other. Gus behind at first, then ahead, restless, almost like a dog that wanders here and there while its owners walk a simple yet boring straight line. Green thought about what they must look like to an outsider. A stereotypical family unit. Man, woman, child. There had been a time when Green had thought he would have that in his life. A woman. A family. Somehow life had gone on and time had passed and the things he had wanted, thought that he'd wanted, had not come about. The strange thing about it was how normal it had felt. He couldn't quite put his finger on it. The longing. The disappointment. The unfulfilled desires. Now it felt almost impossible to imagine his life any other way. He had no inkling that this outing was anything but friendly, yet it tapped into that submerged longing he had not thought of in many years, a dormant riverbed damp with the first trickles of snowmelt.

They sat on a bench at the park and watched Gus play on the swings. Patches of fresh snow withered beneath the sun and everything was wet and glowed in the midday light. Green felt a moment of guilt as Gus ran off with a smile on his face. Of course he wanted to see the boy at ease, but there was still the school suspension. The afternoon was panning out to be more like a fun day off than anything resembling castigation. Maybe the boy needed the break, he told himself.

How'd you end up being a priest?

Well, said Green, I'm a pastor, not a priest, but that's alright. To a lot of people there probably doesn't seem like much of a difference.

Sorry. That's what I meant. I'm not very religious. I get things mixed up, but I do know some things.

Oh, that's alright. No harm done. My father and mother were both pastors in the Lutheran church, and when you have that as a backdrop, I think it becomes less of something you choose to do and more a question of whether you're going to choose not to fall into the family business or just let it happen, so to speak.

That makes sense. I've heard that said about doctors too. Maybe lawyers. Can't say I've met too many pastors in my life.

It's a career path.

It's more than a career, I would think. Kind of a life's dedication.

Green thought for a moment. Watched Gus swinging on the monkey bars. There were other kids about but all much younger than he, not yet school age.

No more so than any other career or lifestyle, I suppose. What you do takes an immense dedication.

Well, yes, but . . .

What?

I was going to say that people's lives are greatly influenced by your profession, more so than mine, what with morals and just how people live their day-to-days. Then I remembered that technically speaking, I deal with life-and-death stuff on a daily basis.

That's true.

Doesn't always feel like that though. I think the death

part is always lingering just out of sight, and I've become desensitized to it over the years. I still get sad when any of the residents move on, but it's inevitable. It's why they're there. Essentially to die.

Or have the best possible end-of-life experience.

I wish that were true. Old folks' homes are sad places. Ours is alright. At least folks get the care they need in there. That's not true across the board though. There's a lot of shadiness in that business, for whatever reason.

Makes sense to me.

Deb looked taken aback. Why is that? she said.

Because it's a product of man. Or, well, humans.

Deb eyed him with a narrow stare.

I'm sorry, said Green. I didn't mean to turn pessimistic on you.

No, now I'm curious. Go on.

Well, I don't know. I guess I've gotten a little jaded. Why would God make it so things like that happen to good people? There's a lot of ugliness in the world. I guess it just doesn't shock me the way it used to. In a way I've come to expect it.

I thought you were supposed to, I don't know, have, like, answers or something. Or at least paint a pretty picture or encourage the goodness in folks.

I'm done encouraging. Just telling it like it is. Anymore the pretty picture feels like a dream. We all have to wake up at some point.

Across the playground a toddler screamed for its mother. A semi roared past on the adjacent highway, faster than it should have been going through town. They sat on the bench not talking. The magic of the day faded.

I'm sorry, said Green. I shouldn't have said that stuff.

Why not?

He shrugged. I don't know.

Well, it's better than lying, said Deb. But, can I ask you a question?

You just did.

Well, another question.

Sure. Shoot.

Why do you still do it?

Do what?

What you do. Pastoring. Give guidance you don't believe in.

I never said I don't believe it. I'm just . . . He trailed off, recognizing the contradiction he'd made.

Deb was silent until Green turned his head and looked at her. Lowered his gaze. Well, he said. Fiddled with his fingers. Traced the pleat in his ironed black pants. Could think of nothing more to say.

It was a quiet walk back across town. A quiet drive north. Gus was tired. That was good. He'd sleep tonight. Green was also tired but knew that sleep would not come so easy to his spinning mind, and so it was. Long into the night the words echoed in his head, back and forth and all around. *Why do you still do it? Give guidance you don't believe in.* She was right, and that was a valid question. One of the many questions he could not answer.

Tom

•

TOM HORAK LEFT HOME AT SIXTEEN AND DID NOT return for a full calendar year. Then one morning in early autumn, his mother, Bethany Horak-Sainger, answered the telephone and it was her son. Said he'd be up later that afternoon, and around two thirty or so she looked down the road and there he was, puttering up the three-mile line of gravel that snaked along the hay meadow in a rusted-out Toyota 4Runner. When he pulled up in the yard, the morphed shadow of the vehicle in the angled sun, his mother was standing in the parted screen door of the kitchen. She stepped down from the stoop and greeted him midway between the house and his car.

He'd grown in the year's absence, she could see that. They hugged and she stepped back, saying, Let me get a look at you. Don't you ever stop growin? She smiled up at him.

Dark greasy hair covered her son's neck. A thin beard with bare patches between his sideburns and mouth. Wisp of a mustache brushed over his upper lip. He smelled of body odor and his jaw hung low, lips parted, as if always on the verge of speaking. Faded jeans worn to white horizontal thread on one knee. Sneakers. Stained blue flannel tucked in at the waist. The tucked-in shirt was the only thing about him that appeared put together, and his mother wondered if it was for her sake or something that he always did. When he was younger she had the luxury of dressing him and then later telling him, or at least giving her opinion on, how he ought to dress. Now she knew those days were gone. She followed him into the house, urging him ahead of her.

His father sat at the table. Freshly perked coffee and pie made from apples they'd brought back from Delta County on a day trip along with a load of firewood from his mother's kin that still lived over there and owned an orchard. Standing as the screen door slapped shut behind them, the man looked at his son from across the small room and said, kind of timid, Well? You goin a give your old man a hug?

Tom walked around the table. His father made no move to go to him. Wrapped their arms around each other. The son held back, not fully committed to the hug. An involuntary reflex at the closeness of the man. They sat and his mother poured coffee.

You workin? his father asked after a few moments of silence interspersed by clinking spoons mixing in the sugar and half-and-half.

Tom swallowed a bite of pie. Washed it down with a sip of the cheap coffee his parents drank. It tasted awful, the acrid liquid sliding down his throat, unsettling his gut.

I'm workin construction, he said.

His father crossed his arms, leaned back in his chair. The joints in the legs moaned with the shift in weight.

What sort of construction?

And I work at a restaurant.

What?

I also work at a restaurant.

Two jobs. That's good, I guess.

We're buildin some condos right now. Up by the ski resort.

Hmm. Those fuckin things. What do you do at the restaurant?

I'm at the dive station.

His father squinted at him, so Tom clarified, I wash dishes.

Tom Sr. only stared. A look of disgust.

The mother flashed a look at her husband. Said, Where are you livin? Is it a nice place?

I crashed on a friend's couch last winter. Mostly lived out of my car once it got warm enough.

The mother, a sharp intake of breath.

Campin, he went on, ruminating. Not a bad way to spend a summer.

You can't live outta your car in the winter, his mother said.

Tom shook his head. Looked at the ceiling. Groaned.

I know that, Mom. I'm movin in with Rust. We got a place in town we're rentin.

A long silence. Early evening crept through the windows, the hills cast in a yellow-orange light. His mother asked, Have you met any girls?

I've met lots of people.

You know what I mean. She reached out and grabbed him by the wrist, shaking it playfully.

I'm not datin anyone, he said, which was technically true. Not telling them he'd spent every night of the last two weeks with one of the waitresses from the restaurant. It wasn't a lie because they hadn't told anyone, not even at the restaurant. Keeping it a secret because that made it more exciting, made the sex better. Tension building throughout the day, released at night in a dark room filled with giggles, whimpers, moans, the sound their naked bodies made moving against each other. And besides, they were just having fun. Hadn't put a name yet to whatever it was they were doing. And here Tom thought, as if for the first time, *There are things I don't want them to know about me, and not just pertaining to sex.* He smiled at his secret, at the very thought of having a secret. Sugar on his tongue. Took a sip of coffee. The bitter drink gone cold.

I need to grab some of my stuff.

Well, his mother said, pressing her hands on her thighs and yawning, you'll have to dig it out of the closet. I put everything in there so I could use your room to sew.

Seeing the worried look on her son's face, she said, Don't worry, it's all there. And I tried not to snoop.

The feet of his chair vibrated on the linoleum. His parents glanced at each other. His father spoke.

When you're done there's somethin me and your mom need to talk to you about. It's important.

Tom barely registered the words as he took the stairs two at a time.

In the closet of his bedroom his belongings were stacked in boxes, shirts hung from wire hangers on the wooden bar that stretched from wall to wall. He rummaged through the items and containers until he found a box that contained green rubber-coated binoculars. An antler-handled Buck knife in a leather sheath slatted to fit on a belt. Another leather case with the disassembled pieces of a bone saw. Small rectangular sharpening stone. He put the box back and looked at his things. His childhood, shuttered away in storage. Some clothes, neatly folded. A tall box with posters rolled up and bound by rubber bands. Dinged cigar box filled with trinkets. He opened it. Feathers. One large, striped dark brown and speckled white from the tail of a turkey. Another from the wing of a red-tailed hawk, drifted down to him when the raptor had taken off from the pole of a power line while he craned his neck to look. He'd taken it as sign of good fortune and held on to the feather. Piece of bone the size of his thumb, flared on one end, petrified sponge interior where the marrow had rotted and dried like wormholes worn down below some joint or socket. Chipped fragment of volcanic glass. A chunk of limestone with the fluted cones of rugose coral, round eyes of crinoid stems like fossilized kaleidoscopes. This wasn't what he'd come for, nothing in the cigar box was of any actual use, but now looking at it, he had a strong desire never to part with it again. He closed the lid and tucked it under his arm.

Standing to leave he noticed the table on the south wall below the window. Padded chair pushed in. Heavy black sewing machine threaded with a spool of yellow. A strip of cloth punctured by downcast needle striated with test strips of a variety of stitching patterns. The bed was made with a flowered spread and his mother's pillows. Her Bible on the little table below a silver lamp. He walked to the bedside table and pulled open the top drawer. Found there the dropper bottle of melatonin she used as a sleep aid and beside it a smattering of pill bottles. He picked them up one at a time and read the labels. Prescriptions to his mother's name. Capecitabine. Gabapentin. Morphine. Another one he could not pronounce that was to be used to quell nausea. So many others. Set them each back in the drawer bottom and walked down the stairs feeling every step, some new anxiety rising. Could not recall his mother being one to take many medications. He pushed back against it, let it sink before rounding the corner into the living room at the bottom of the stairs.

His mother and father at the table. Through the window above the sink, a gray evening. Purpling sky. He stood in the empty doorframe that bore the progress of generations, the boy's height etched in yearly increments beside those of his father, his father's siblings.

What's that? his father asked him, looking at the cigar box.

Huntin stuff.

You huntin this year?

Why wouldn't I?

I don't know. That's your business.

Tom could not come to grips with something. The pills in the bedside table had rattled him, and he was not sure what to make of it. More than that, though, was something to do with his father's demeanor. He was still a hard man, but the sharpness of his words had softened some. As if he was holding back the bitterness that had consumed him in Tom's earlier years. He could not square it. His body braced for an impact that appeared unlikely to come. His mother shifted in her chair, hands clasped on her lap beneath the table.

You usin the cabin?

We were thinkin of settin a camp over the pass along Willow Creek, or thereabouts.

Eyes widened, arms crossed with a forearm extending vertical, chin cradled between thumb and forefinger. That's big country, Tom Sr. said.

You hunted over there before?

Oh ya.

Elk?

Mm-hmm.

It was growing dark out. Night settled over the place. His mother stifled a yawn. Rose, groaned, and placed her hand on her lower back as she flipped the overhead light on then crossed the kitchen and pulled from the fridge a platter with a whole chicken wreathed by chunks of carrot and potato. Set it on the cold stove and lit the oven.

Who you huntin with?

Rust.

His father grunted.

After a while Tom said, I better get goin.

Both his parents looked dumbfounded and hurt by this announcement.

Aren't you stayin for dinner? his mother said. I thawed a chicken.

I've got work early tomorrow. I need to get back.

Still leaning in the doorway, tightness in his upper back. He righted his posture, stretched against the tension. His father said, Just stay for dinner, son. There's somethin your mother and I need to talk to you about.

I can't. I need to get back. Just goin to grab my rifle.

His father stared him down. Suit yourself, he said. You know where it's at. Key's in the same spot.

They said their last goodbyes and his mother sat at the table, exhausted. Tom walked down to the barn. It was quiet in the yard. The chickens had roosted and mostly shut up for the night. A lowing of cows in the upper pasture. In the barn he found the key hung on a nail below the workbench and he unlocked the storage room and pulled the cord dangling from the ceiling light. Stood there as his eyes adjusted. Tried not to think about what he'd seen in his room. His mother's room.

Around him were shelves containing all manner of objects. Pieces of hydraulic systems cannibalized off broken-down machines. On one wall hung his father's horse tack. One entire line of shelving was devoted to coffee cans filled with different nails, screws, bolts, and nuts and any other small piece of hardware that might come in handy but would likely sit on that shelf for something resembling eternity. He walked to one corner and stood before the gun safe. Opened it. The locking mechanism had never worked as far as anyone could remember, but his father was old-fashioned anyhow. Didn't take to keeping them under lock and key. The lock on the door to the storage room had been his compromise, there for the guns as much as anything else in that room, mostly the power tools that were stowed under the work bench marked by scrapes and holes and burn marks. There were about a dozen long-barreled guns leaned up along the back of the safe, and he went through them until he found the .30-.06 he'd hunted with in the past. It had been a year or two since he'd shot it. Had always been a good shot. He also took a 12-gauge shotgun that his father had given him for his fourteenth birthday. Then he turned off the light and walked out into the yard. As he approached the 4Runner, he looked up at the house. Through the kitchen window he could see his parents locked in an embrace. His mother's face was buried in her husband's shoulder. His father looked up and through the window made eye contact, arms draped over his wife's back. A sad smile and his face was wet. That was the only time he could recall seeing his father cry. The juxtaposition with the man that he thought he knew was jarring. Tom had not thought his father capable of tears, of any kind of tender emotion, so he buried it. Chalked it up as a one-off, though the thought of the medications, the conversation his parents had wanted to have, lingered. Haunted him as he drove out down the gravel road, his mind on a woman, the warmth of a bed, the sex-charged freedom of young lust passed off as love, and he longed to disappear.

•

Tom stood in the barn on the now-vacant ranch and thought of those long-ago days. Wondered what his father would think of him now. Didn't want to know what his mother would have to say. He'd never really lived up to any of their expectations of him, what he thought those expectations were. He had always told himself that when he had kids, he would be a different kind of father. A different kind of man. He'd never had to cross that bridge and at this point likely never would. Thought about his distant mother. Always felt he had disappointed her, though she was never one to lay any kind of criticism on her son. He had always viewed her as a passive woman, had even come to resent that in her at different times in his life, though now when he thought of it, he couldn't say why he'd been prone to that bent. Perhaps it foreboded hitherto unforetold shit that he had yet to unearth and deal with. The things folks carried with them without ever thinking or knowing about. Maybe that's why he'd ended up the way he did, but he didn't believe that. There was the one, the woman, the one that got away. The one that dragged him down alongside her until he'd sucked himself dry of anything resembling a thriving manhood. *Manhood.* He sneered. What had that ever got him? He'd been ushered into various rites of passage that the rural white heterosexual male seemed to value above almost everything else. Whether it had been work—*grinders find a way*—or hunting—*that'll make a man out of you*—or something as juvenile as a sip of whiskey—*it'll put hair on yer chest.* And of course sex. He couldn't think of any saying to go with that other than *gettin some*. He'd gone through that phase. Maybe he'd never grown out of it. Lust. That sin that is always on the tip of every man's tongue if not a different body part. Maybe you grew out of it as you got older and your libido shriveled up and all but fell off. Tom was of the opinion that it wasn't just men that dealt with all that, though maybe they were weaker against it. He thought a lot of men looked straight past a woman's desires to the image of her that they'd already formulated in their minds before ever meeting her. That or they passed it off as loose morals, labeled her easy, perhaps a slut. Some term to let her know without ever having to say that they did not approve. He'd always considered himself different from other men, but was that the truth of it? The one that got away, he'd called her those things and worse inside his mind, never saying out loud the names he wanted to. But she had wronged him. She deserved it. She was all those things and more, and he'd shunted himself lower than any man he'd derided through tongue or thought.

·

THE WOMAN, OR *THAT* WOMAN, AS HIS MOTHER would come to call her. Name of Rosa Lynne. Called Rose by her family, introduced herself as such. Hair like fireweed twine. The soul of a gypsy.

They worked together at the restaurant. That's how they met, and it began with a dinner at her house with friends. Lingering as each left, until it was only them. She asked if he wanted another beer. He said sure, and when that was done, Do you want to go to my room?

They sat on the edge of the bed and kissed. Soft, wet lips. He put his hands under her shirt to feel the warmth of her belly and she lifted her arms so he pulled it over her head. A white cotton bra hung loose on her small breasts set wide on her chest. She removed this without his help.

On their sides in nothing but their drawers, he drew his fingers over the only fabric she wore. She brushed his. Said, Let me help you with that, and curled down and put her mouth on him.

Weeks later, after they'd settled into a sort of routine, occasional hikes during the days they had off together, nights of losing themselves in each other's bodies, the long mornings after when they felt they could stay in bed all day, his head on her chest, she said, The lines are blurred with you.

What do you mean?

Between fucking, having sex, and making love. The lines are blurred.

He didn't know what she meant and so said nothing.

She was like that, difficult to size up or pin down. There were so many things about her that were difficult for him to understand. Maybe that's what kept him coming back. The shroud she carried over herself. He longed to see through it. Most of the time he felt he hardly knew her.

Soon they began to fight. She'd go cold at a moment's notice. Took offense at little things. He got out of bed before she did in the morning and she wouldn't talk to him for the rest of the day. She made plans to go out with a friend and he didn't call her for a week until he woke at night and there she was beside him with no clothes on and she put his hand between her legs and like that they were back in each other's lives. Stars fixed in elliptic gravitational waltz, always with that focal point of the physicality between them, coming close and then slung out again to the farthest reaches of orbit. Drawn together with each passing. Unaware of the fierce pull of the black hole at the center that would consume both when the space between them had vanished.

It happened out Willow Creek. A backpacking trip they'd been planning for a month, the long weekend set aside, shifts covered to make time. It began even before they'd left. While packing he told her not to forget condoms, and she said, What if I did? Would that ruin the trip for you? He hesitated and said, I'm sure we'd find a way around it. She laughed. A single, forced exhale. He said, What, and she went silent for the remainder of the morning.

At the trailhead she threw her pack on and disappeared into the trees while he was still lacing his boots.

After moving to town, Tom had lost the bit of a drawl that he'd grown up speaking with and that was common in the ranching community in those parts, coming out only when he was around the folks he'd grown up with. He yelled after her.

Do you even know where you're going?

Caught up a mile into the hike. Followed at a close distance, hoping she'd speak first.

A while later, You just walk off like that?

No response but the rhythmic scrape of feet.

Will you at least talk to me?

Okay. I'm talking. Voice level, emotionless.

What if we got separated? How would I find you?

It's a trail. You just follow the trail.

Ya, but you've never been up here. And there are other trails. How am I supposed to know where you went? What's the point of going backpacking together if we're not going to do it together?

You don't trust me to wait for you at an intersection. It wasn't a question.

I don't know. Maybe. Can we just talk about these things?

We're talking now. What do you want to talk about? Your insecurity?

Hey.

How you don't trust me?

I trust you.

No you don't. You just said you didn't. Anger in her voice now.

Tom sighed. Said in a soft voice, I don't want to fight.

That quiet exhaling laugh. Just because we're fighting doesn't mean we're not talking.

Ya, but every time we try to talk we end up fighting.

The trail forked in a hollow of evergreens. Rose stopped and turned around.

Doesn't that worry you? he said, almost pleading.

Worry me how?

I mean, is this the kind of relationship you want?

She squinted at him, her mouth tightening. What are you saying?

He began to fidget, hands moving. Looked away from her. I'm not saying anything. I mean. Are you happy?

She was quiet, then said, I want to be with you. If I didn't I wouldn't be here.

Silence. Faint trickle of water. A whistling breeze in the high boughs.

Do you want to be with me? Her voice grew small, all the anger gone out of it. Replaced by something else, a little fear. Vulnerability.

He took a moment, staring at her eyes, those blue crystal eyes.

I don't know, he said.

He dropped his gaze. They stood, a sinking in his chest. The world felt hollow. Trees mocked him. After a time he asked, Are you okay?

I don't want to talk right now.

Do you want to go back?

She shifted her weight, pack sidling behind her.

No.

Okay, he said, allowing himself a weak smile. You can keep leading. If you want to.

She laughed, a genuine reaction from the pit of her diaphragm, absent of bitterness. I don't know which way, she said, and he started down the left-hand fork without another word.

That evening Tom cooked a meal of ramen with bits of salami floating in the broth. He'd made a kitchen area under a large spruce downwind from the tent. Rose had gone down the rise below camp, the sharp slope butted up against the bench where the tent was set. She lay on the hill and he carried the steaming pot to her with two spoons.

Hungry?

At first she didn't move, her eyes closed. He felt resentment begin to surface, had turned to leave when she finally sat up and acknowledged him.

Are you hungry?

She said that she was and he passed her the pot, said, Just save me half. Sat in the grass beside her with a little space between them.

They ate. Watched the angle of trees across the narrow valley. Evening fell. A rustling noise. A buck, grazing up below the trail, stepped into view not twenty yards before them. They went still. The animal lowered its head and ate. Took a step. Ate again. Moved steadily closer. Ten yards now. Tom could hear Rose's slow, shallow breath, and he knew she was willing herself into complete silence, to blend in with the grass and the breeze, as he was. The direction of the wind and the shadowed slope was to their advantage. The buck grazed in the last bit of light cast from the west at their backs. Five yards. Close enough that Tom felt he could leap out from where he sat and latch on to the beast, wrestle it to the ground or else ride it, let it carry him deep into wilderness. The sound of Rose's breathing made him think of something he'd heard about mountain lions, how they would crouch near the borders of shadows so that prey coming from sun into darkness would not see them as their eyes adjusted to the change in light. It stepped closer, then jerked its head up and stared at him, sifting through shapes in the scant light. Tom tried to envision what it saw. Motionless stones with eyes, materialized out of nothing. The buck snorted, a loud, quick burst of air from its snout that made both of them jump as it bounded gracefully away over a bend in the land and was gone.

Something warm in his palm. He looked and Rose had taken his hand. They sat for a long time, into full dark. Cool air falling. Individual stars winked into existence as the dregs of the day faded into the west.

Later in the tent it was like having sex with a familiar stranger. The scent and touch they knew so well, yet there was some element of otherness to it. Everything with a force behind it, an energy of fear and anger and survival. He went down on her and she held him by the back of the head, writhing the bone of her pelvis against his face and chin. He felt like he was fighting something, trying to restrain without hurting. He pressed his way up her torso and kissed her, sucking at her lip, and she bit him and he cried out. She rolled him over and straddled him, hips bucking, screaming, gripped him by the hair on his chest and he lay there, watching whatever it was that had grown up between them, some terrifying mountain spirit exercised by the wails and moans, the frantic grind and slap of their bodies. She climaxed before he did and collapsed in a pulsing lump of hair and skin, gasping breath in his ear like a high wheeze, body trembling, then heaving, and an onset of moisture in his neck. Deep, full-bodied sobs. He held her, squeezed her to him. Pulled the sleeping bags over them to absorb their warmth. After a time her body stilled. A soft weeping, then only breathing.

He slipped from beneath her. Sat up and zipped their sleeping bags together. Then lay with her back to him, arm draped over her middle. Bristled hair tucked in the quick of his chin. Woke with the sun warming the inside of the tent. Rose was sitting up beside him looking dazed. He put his hand on the small of her back and she stroked the hair on his stomach. A slim, cold smile. Withdrew her hand. Said, I think we should go home. And then, I want to go home.

Ya, he said.

She put her arms into the sleeves of a thin wool shirt, light blue. There was stubble in her armpits as she slipped it over her shoulders, the point of her breast, rounded flesh bunched at the bottom of her ribcage. She never looked him in the eye. When she'd fully dressed he couldn't help feeling like something had been lost, either between them or to him alone, he couldn't tell, just that he'd once known something and would never know that thing again.

They packed up camp and walked the long way back to the car. Never speaking. He dropped her off at her house and went home alone. Showered, and though it was midday, he crawled into bed and buried himself beneath the heavy blankets and pillows.

Rust and Tom were living together when his relationship with Rose fell apart, and the falling apart was messy. They'd only dated for a few months, though to Tom it felt like an eternity. His longest relationship to date. There was some semblance of an attempt at friendship, though friendship did not come easy to the former lovers. Rose was flirtatious by nature, her default around certain men, a fallback when uncomfortable, which she always was around Tom. Tom took it personally. Every smile flashed his way hid unspoken desire. When she talked with men at the restaurant, he felt those words were meant for him and he hated the recipient of her flirtations as much as he loathed the source. They still slept together occasionally, falling into old habits. An on-again, off-again sort of thing that lasted another few months. He woke after those incidents in a state of loss, his insides bound in stone. Then she stopped coming around and Tom did what he always did when at a loss. Retreated to nature. The cool warmth of autumn. Winds shifting out of the north. Daylong woods rambles with small tokes of pot throughout. He looked for secrets in the woods, some part of himself hidden in the roots and bedrock, cultivated in soil. Watched elk in the evenings. Came to know their habits, their routines. Noted when the rut faded sometime in October, weather turned cold, and they gathered in herds put on the move when the storms built.

He and Rust shot a cow on Willow Creek during second

rifle and packed it out in a blizzard, butchering by the warmth of a woodstove as the days grew short.

Then it was winter and the nights were long and Rose was around again. They shared meals, the three of them, Tom and Rose and Rust. Rose would spend the night on the couch, only occasionally putting her hand down the front of his pants when they huddled under blankets to watch movies after Rust had gone to bed.

Tom savored those moments, held tight the ecstasy as a barrier to shame. Used it as a guard when he began to hear the sounds of lovemaking through the wall he shared with Rust's bedroom. Said nothing when she appeared in the morning wearing only a translucent white shirt.

He watched their relationship blossom like a festering wound. Tom and Rose had been broken up for some time, the better part of half a year, but with the on-again, off-again phase it felt like no time at all. Tom experienced a kind of loathing glee when Rust and Rose would argue, thinking that they deserved each other. Covetous when they made up and went through periods of joy that excluded him. Maybe the half-in approach to dating was just something Rose did.

Then there was the time that Rust left town and she stayed over anyway. The two of them alone in the house. Standing in the kitchen with a cup of tea, she held an aloof expression he took for sadness, and, without asking, he gently took the mug from her hands and hugged her.

She exhaled into him, put her arms around his waist, face turned sideways on his chest. Hands creeping up and his fingers in her hair, shaky breath. She felt his heart quicken. Said, No. Softly, Stop. Then pushed him away and left him standing there, hot tea cooling on the counter.

That night when she climbed naked into his bed he lay on his back with his arms resting on the mattress. On her side, she took his hand, kissed it, trailed the tips of his fingers over a cold stiffened nipple. Placed it between her legs. He let her turn his palm as she slid his fingers where she wanted them. Applied pressure when her breath deepened and her hips rocked until she shuddered and stopped. When she used her mouth to take care of him he only lay back and let it happen, and in the morning when she crawled from his bed he pretended to sleep. Woke and saw that the door to the adjacent bedroom was closed. He ate a breakfast of cold cereal, packed a lunch, and left for work.

Rose and Rust moved fast. The courtship lasted only a year before they got married. Tom attended the wedding but was not involved in any meaningful way. He and Rust had grown apart in that time. He kept to the peripheries. Ate dinner. Had a couple beers and left early, alone.

After the wedding Tom spent a week at the cabin. Hikes during the day, lengthy walks to places he'd always known. Long periods of stillness. Prostrate on the ground, head up on a log. Eyes closed in the warm sun. Then back to the cabin to chop wood, doing everything in his power to exhaust himself before sundown, when sleep could save him from the unfortunate verities of waking life.

When he returned, their things were gone from the little house where all three had lived together. Rust and Rose moved into a place down valley. The vacant room held a mix of their smells. Dust on a white windowsill. The long silent nights.

He saw them little after the move. Dinner a few times a year. Some gatherings, more around the holidays and in summer. Mostly though, Tom lived a solitary life. Dated a few women, nothing serious. Met them at bars or parties. At first older, and then, as he aged, younger than himself. First encounters always involved a few drinks. Heavy flirting in rooms with low lights and loud music, leaning close to shout in each other's ears, cheeks brushing, then falling into the night before falling into bed. Few words. No emotion.

He held low opinions of the women he took home, an externalization of how he thought of himself. Short-lived affairs of sporadic frequency, less and less over time until days turned to months, and then years passed since he'd been with a woman.

In all that time Tom rarely went home. Distracted by vice and lust. Crutch upon crutch. Periodic calls from his father telling him to visit his mother. That bastard was the last one Tom wanted telling him what to do. Though his father had changed some, no longer held sway over Tom, he could not forgive him for the things he'd done in Tom's early childhood. The bullying. The constant bullshit. The abuse. He fantasized what it would be like to be estranged from the man. Instead, he latched on to a lingering hatred.

It was late in the summer of his thirtieth year when Rose called. Some years after she and Rust had married. Asked if he'd go for a hike, a walk at least. Rust was out of town. She needed to get out of the house. Suggested his parents' property. It had been so long since she'd been up there.

He drove, she in the passenger seat with the window down. Haying season. Winding contoured lines left by the swather. The musky scent of fresh cuttings. Going slow, watching her out of the corner of his vision stare out at something, the sky. Sullen smile at a passing thought.

Tom felt the loss of his mother. Had heard that the cancer was running its course. Killing her. Didn't want to see her in that state. But an urge drove him to head up to the house. His father's truck was not there. He asked Rose to stay in the car. Walked up to the house and went inside.

The house was quiet. Was anyone there? A faint hello beckoned from the second story. He walked up the stairs, every step creaking beneath his weight. Found his mother in bed in his old room. He went in and stood, silent.

Tom, she said. This is such a nice surprise. What are you doin here?

Her voice was faint. Skin pale and sallow. She was frail. It broke his heart to see her like this and for a moment he regretted coming to visit her.

Oh I don't know, said Tom. I just . . . He trailed off. Unsure what to say.

Come here, his mother said. Sit down.

Tom walked forward and took a seat at the edge of the bed. Timid.

It's been so long, she said. I didn't think you were goin to visit anymore.

No, he said. I just . . . I don't know.

Tom looked down. He didn't want to look his mother in the eye. Thought she might see something there, something he didn't want to show her. Every one of his shortcomings.

It's okay, she said, always forgiving. Come closer.

Tom slid along the bed until his mother reached out and took his hand. Squeezed it in a meek grip.

Now tell me, she said. Where have you been? What have you been up to?

Tom was quiet. Mumbled, Not much. Workin and livin, I guess. Normal stuff.

His mother stared at him. Labored breath. A blank, discerning gaze.

163

I didn't think I'd ever see you again, she said. I don't think I'll be around much longer. I don't know how much . . .

She coughed and reached for a balled-up tissue on the bed beside her. Spit into it and folded it, setting it back on the bed.

I don't how much time I have left. Not much if you believe the doctors. This damn cancer. I'm sorry you have to see me like this.

Tom was sorry too but didn't say it. It felt shallow and callous even to think it. His mother's eyes dipped, like she was going to fall asleep. She held them closed for a time, breathed, more of a wheeze than actual breath.

You don't have to say anythin, she said. I wish your father were here. He would have liked to see you. I'm not sure when he'll be back.

Tom's anger surged at the thought his father. He did not want to see him. Could not see how his mother would think to say such a thing. Why would he want to see that man? Given their history. His mother's forgiving nature could be her finest grace as well as her greatest flaw. Blind to what Tom had been through. Or maybe willfully ignorant. Denial.

Tom wanted to say something, not knowing what. Like there should be the perfect phrase that would sum everything up. Everything he was feeling. A lifetime of feelings bottled into a few words. There was no such phrase.

I'm so tired all the time, his mother said. It's these damn drugs they have me on. Almost want to quit them altogether. Don't know that I could bear it though. It's like somethin's eatin me from the inside.

Her eyes closed again. Tom watched her. She looked almost peaceful, if not for the sickly visage she held. He was grateful for the silence. Nothing more he could possibly say. Soon he could see that she was asleep. He rose and pulled the covers up under her armpits, limbs atop the bedspread. He felt tears well up. Did not allow any to shed. He stood in the hallway and composed himself. Didn't want Rose to seem him this way. When he felt stable he went downstairs and out into the yard. Got in the truck and did not say anything.

How's she doing? Rose asked as they pulled out of the yard.

Fine, he said. Lied. Nothing was fine. Not in the literal sense of it.

Is she really sick?

Tom did not respond. Drove down the road. He tried not to think of his parents. The guilt trip his father would lay on him. Again, his mother as he did not want to remember her. He looked at Rose, the beautiful woman that still held his heart, cast about like a stone in water, perhaps skipping for a moment, yet always sinking. Felt the tears well again. Let her smile and soft features mask the void he could not fill. He looked away.

He parked the 4Runner in a wide spot on the road below the house and they got out. Walked through the sagebrush in the hazy afternoon. Sat on a hillock overlooking the meadow, knees drawn in. Tom looked out at the road and the meadow beneath them, the machinery parked in the center where his father had left it for the day.

I'm sorry, said Rose.

What for? Tom wasn't sure where this was going. Try as he could, he could not stop thinking about his mother.

She stared hard at him. You're going to make me say it, aren't you?

Say what? He smiled, a sad smile.

I never meant for it to happen the way it did. With Rust.

Tom's body stiffened. He hadn't been sure what to expect, but that wasn't it. It caught him off guard.

He misses you, she said. I miss you.

She moved closer, put her hand on his.

There was something Tom wanted to say to this but he couldn't figure out what it was. He'd always coveted Rose and resented Rust for what had happened between them.

She put her head on his shoulder. Tears soaked the collar of his shirt. Then she was kissing him on the neck and he closed his eyes, insides twisting like a high ringing in the center of his torso. She put her hand on his cheek, turned his face toward her, and kissed him on the mouth, the salt of her crying, and he took a deep, involuntary

166

breath. She put his earlobe between her lips, whispered, I'm sorry.

Tom kissed her neck. Moved around to her face and kissed her on the lips, hands on her body. Then it began. Hands slipped beneath clothing. They operated on impulse. Not thinking of anything. She sat astride him, and as they made love, Tom allowed relief to flow through him for the first time in years. Everything was perfect. Until it was finished. He held her to him. Caressed her hair. Took in the smell of her. Tender kisses and a feeling of ecstasy, but nothing was reciprocated. She'd gone cold. Rolled away from him and did not speak.

As they drove down the road there was silence. Rose stared out the window. Ahead he saw dust rising and a truck coming up the narrow road. His father's truck. He sank. A hollow feeling in his chest. As he neared, the truck pulled over and he saw the window roll down. Saw the face of the man that was more shocked than anything, a light smile that was out of place from the image of his father that he held in his mind. The smile shifted as Tom drove past without slowing. Caught the change in expression out the periphery of his vision, something like sadness. A disappointment that Tom draped over himself. He didn't want to see anymore, know anymore. Sped away. Not looking at Rose. Told himself he didn't care what she thought of him. He blocked out the world, a hardening that seeped inward. Willed himself not to glance in the rearview mirror.

The following spring. Tom walking up the street. A few puddles from the melting snow and a warm wind come up in the late morning. He'd taken to walking and often passed by the Hawkins house. Couldn't say why. Tried not to be seen. This day that was not an option. The warm spring morning had drawn folks from their homes. Brought them out into the sun and there was Rose and Rust and the baby on the grass. It was Rose that saw him.

Tom. *Tom*, she yelled.

He tried to ignore her.

Tom!

Stopped. Looked at them. He stood there across the street before lowering his head and moving over toward the yard. He stood on the edge of the property and looked up at the sun, the light on his unshaven face. Lowered his gaze and there was Rust. They looked at each other.

Come meet the little one, said Rose.

Tom walked on the grass until he stood above them. Rust looked up.

Hey, Tom.

Hey.

This is Gus, said Rose. Say hi, Gus. Her voice a high-pitched baby talk. The infant lay there, arms and legs flailing. Such a tiny thing. Tom's insides twisted at the sight of it. An emotion he did not have a name for. Mix of fear and jealousy, the undercurrents of rage. Felt a panic rise inside of him.

How are things? Rust asked.

Alright, said Tom, feigning calm and his country accent coming out.

A long silence interspersed by Rose's baby-talk ramblings and the cooing of the actual baby.

Boy? said Tom.

Huh?

It's a boy.

Yeah, said Rust. Gus is a boy's name.

Sure is.

Long silence. Tom only felt capable of small talk, and barely even that.

We should get together sometime, said Rose.

Yeah, said Tom, not believing that it would ever happen. That would be good, he said.

A longer silence.

Go on in the house and fetch Tom a beer, Rust said to Rose. She was sitting on the ground hovering over the baby. Did not answer. Hey, said Rust, nudged her with his foot. She looked up, away from her son. I said go get Tom a beer.

She hesitated. I'm all good, said Tom.

Rust stared at Rose. Said, Go on.

Really, said Tom, but Rose stood and disappeared into the house.

The two men stared at the baby like it was some alien object. Tom took in its appearance. Looking at it, the facial features, there was no denying that this a was a Hawkins boy. He had his father's cheekbones, the shape of the eyes and chin, but Tom remembered the afternoon with Rose on the ranch when he'd let himself go. Did some quick math in his head. It didn't quite add up, not without something extraordinary, but Tom ignored that. It was not a conscious decision or even unwillingness. He was simply incapable of accepting what his eyes beheld. Gus would never be his son, legally or biologically, but he could not bring himself to see it that way. If he'd been more self-aware he would have known then that he would always see Gus as his own. The covetous seed planted deep within him. Rust did not deserve what he had, what Tom knew the man took for granted. This family. A wife and son. It should have been his, Tom's. He could not let it go, and a loathing toward Rust burned in his throat.

How's life? said Rust, not looking away from the baby.

Fine.

Just fine?

Tom shrugged. I get along, he said.

Well, hey, said Rust. I been meanin to tell ya for some time. I hope you don't got no hard feelins toward me and Rose.

Tom said nothing. Looked out at the hills across the highway.

It's just . . . uh . . . one a those things, ya know?

Mm-hmm.

A long time passed and then Tom said through gritted teeth, I need to get goin.

Well, said Rust, guess you better get goin then.

Neither said another word and Tom walked away, hurrying up the street. After a bit he heard the voices of Rust and Rose in heated discussion and the burning in his throat flared and did not fall. He didn't walk that way again for a long time.

Tom watched the Hawkins family from a distance. When Rose left it did not surprise him, though he did not know the specifics of her departure. Rose had always been what she referred to as a free spirit, and Tom felt that the fact that even children would not tie her down was not out of character for her. Still, he blamed Rust. Must be a terror to live with, and Tom knew a thing or two about difficult fathers. Maybe Rust got what he deserved. Tom certainly believed that. There was almost a part of him that wanted to feel sorry for Rust, left to raise Gus on his own, though that fire was dwindling. Most of the time he only found things to hate in his onetime friend. And then there was Gus. Whenever he thought about him, Tom could only shake his head and seethe.

He saw Rust only in passing. At the grocery store. A

bar. He seemed to be drinking a lot. Tom heard rumors. Things the neighbors heard or saw. A boy left largely to his own devices. Yelling and crashing noises. Somewhat-regular visits from the authorities.

Tom tried to maintain the relationship, at least with Gus. Even took him out hunting with him once when it became apparent that Rust was not in any shape to teach his son to hunt. It was a futile endeavor, resulting in vitriol from Rust. Tom left with nothing but a feeling of alienation. He told himself he did it for the boy's sake, but there was a selfishness to it, an indulgence in fantasy. Willing himself to contemplate what might have been and would never be.

A few years after Rose's departure Tom was driving out of town and saw the boy walking along the highway with his thumb out. It was early evening, long after school would have gotten out. He pulled over.

Hop in, Gus, he called through the rolled-down window. The boy opened the door and climbed in.

What are you doin walkin? You miss the bus or somethin?

No.

Why are you walkin then?

Gus looked out the window. The houses on the edge of town thinned and were replaced by pasture and wetland, the flat valley between the mountains.

My dad was supposed to pick me up.

Where's he at?

Gus only shrugged. They pulled into the little subdivision and he drove slow on the gravel roads, loath to rush. Unsure what to say.

How was school?

The boy made a face. Fine, he said as if it were the most normal conversation he'd ever had, though to Tom it was anything but. Tom tried to fake a casual demeanor. Felt he was failing but the boy appeared unfazed.

You learn anythin new?

Not really.

When he pulled up at the end of the driveway Gus jumped down without a word.

You need anythin? Tom yelled after him.

No, Gus yelled back. Disappeared through the door.

Tom drove over to the Tavern and got a beer and burger to kill time. Drove back and parked up the street and waited. It was a few hours after dark when the beige pickup with the red horizontal stripe took the turn into the driveway, a little fast Tom thought, and came to a halt. He watched Rust get out and take lumbering steps up to the door and disappear the same way his son had. Tom sat a while longer, unsure what to do. There was really nothing to report. As far as he knew, the boy was safe, if a little neglected, but Rust was home now and what would that entail? What sort of mood was he in? Tom sat in the truck until he couldn't stand it. Opened the door and stepped down on the gravel road.

It was a chilly night. Mid-autumn after the leaves had begun to fall but a few patches of color still plastered the hills. He walked up the street and passed the house. Glanced at the front windows as he did. A light inside allowed him to see a small living room and kitchen. No one there. He kept walking. Passed a couple more houses until he came to a vacant lot and he crossed this and dropped down the bank on the far side. It was a steep hillside that fell down to the river and he could hear the water running, a faint gurgle in the dark. The going was difficult as he traversed the hillside. Twice he tripped over either a rock or a bush and fell onto an outstretched arm and rolled a few feet down the hillside before stopping himself. When he came to the Hawkins house he found that he was too far below to be able to see anything through any of the windows other than a thin slit of ceiling. Scrambled up the bank and perched on the corner of the house. Wondered whether the roundabout approach had been necessary. Probably could have walked right through the yard. It was worth it though, on the off chance that Rust might have seen him. That was the last thing he wanted. Didn't care too much about the neighbors other than wanting to avoid any run-ins with police. Or dogs. Now as he thought about it, he hadn't heard any dogs barking. That was something to remember. He made his way to a spot below a window on the north side of the house with a thin trail of light gleaming through the pane. Crouched and rose until he could see a wall beyond and a bed with a small table beside it and a lamp and Gus there in bed. He could not tell if the boy was sleeping or not but he wasn't moving. He watched until he was satisfied that Gus was alright and ducked back down before his luck ran out and the boy opened his eyes or his father came in.

Tom sat leaning against the side of the house. He thought about trying to find Rust but he wasn't sure why outside of pure voyeurism, a means of feeding his resentment. He resisted. Reassured himself that the boy was safe. That was all he needed to sleep that night, but after that day he kept a closer watch on the boy and his father. After Rose's departure, he and Rust had grown more distant and bitter, though he took Gus out for a burger from time to time, playing with his own emotions. On one such occasion he ventured to ask, How's your dad doin?

Gus shrugged. Probably a difficult question for him to answer. Tom often avoided the subject of Rust when talking to Gus. Couldn't say why. In a way he figured if he really wanted to know he could reach out to Rust himself and he wasn't going to do that and so he must not have really wanted to know, which wasn't entirely true. Tom did care. He hoped Rust was miserable.

His primary concern was for Gus. He had resolved to take it upon himself to make sure the boy was cared for, though he wasn't sure how to best go about that. That was when the night prowling escalated. Sometimes he'd park outside the subdivision and take a long walk along the unlit streets. It was a small neighborhood, maybe fifty or sixty houses. He'd go in late, after most of the lights in the houses had gone out. One time, very early in the morning, he got passed by a truck driving very slow and dragging some piece of itself along the gravel beneath the vehicle. The truck had been coming toward him and it stopped and waited for him to walk by before going on. He had a brief thought as he walked past of checking to see if the people in the truck were alright but decided it would be better if he did not get involved. The truck drove off into the night, the singsong scrape of metal ringing through the cold dark air.

Then the prowls became a nightly endeavor. On through the fall and into winter. Tom's personal life suffered. He lost his job on the construction crew. Too many mornings he showed up late or not at all, too sleepy to be of much use. Keeping an eye on the boy became his entire world until one night, the night he should have called the authorities, though it never crossed his mind to do so. He was way past that. Calling the authorities had never been an option to Tom. If it had, he would not have been out there in the middle of the night peeking through windows, yet there he was in his spot on the back of the house thinking about making it up to the windows to take a look, listening to the night and the river in the frozen air, his feet and fingers freezing and his teeth chattering, when a sound broke the stillness. It was a muffled shout followed by a thump and a scream, then silence. He was scrambling his way up the bank when he heard the door open and the truck start. Tires scraping in the frozen gravel, slipping on the ice as Rust lit out down the street. Tom scrambled up the bank and peeked through the window into Gus's room. Saw nothing. Walked around front and hesitated only a moment at the front door before he went inside, closed the door behind him, and spoke into the dark room.

Gus? Gus. Where you at?

No response. He listened. A faint whimper in the dark. He crept through, slow. Followed the sound. Straight back in the hallway behind the kitchen was a door that stood open. A yellow light seeped onto the matted carpet and a shadow of the door slanted on the wall. He poked his head in and saw the boy on the floor in a ball with his face in his hands and his body was shaking. He went to him. Saw on the wall beside him the dent in the Sheetrock and thought about the thump he'd heard after the yelling and before the scream.

Gus. You okay? Tell me what happened.

Gus peeked out from behind his hands. Relaxed a little when he saw who it was and then tensed and donned a look of confusion.

Don't you worry about nothin, said Tom. Don't matter

why I'm here. Only counts that I'm here. Tell me now, are you okay?

Gus rolled over and sat up. I think so, he said.

What happened?

He pushed me.

Tom looked at the boy's head. Let me see here, he said, and he guided Gus's hand away so he could get a better look.

There was a large red lump on the top of his forehead. No blood.

I'm just goin a check it out, Tom said. I just want to make sure of somethin.

He pressed his hands in the area around the bump and the boy winced. He didn't think there was a fracture, but he was no doctor.

You nauseous at all?

What?

Do you feel like you're goin a be sick?

I don't think so.

That's good. How about we get you into bed. It's pretty late. You think you can stand up?

Gus didn't say anything to that but pressed his hands to the carpet and rose to an unstable standing position. Tom held him by the arm and they hobbled down the hall a few feet and into the side bedroom. Tucked him into bed.

I'm a leave now. You think you'll be okay?

Yeah. I think so.

Now you don't tell your dad that I was here, okay? You got that?

Yeah. I won't tell.

Good.

Tom stood and looked at Gus in bed. Was about to leave when Gus asked him, Why are you here, Tom?

Tom wanted to tell him everything. Tell him he loved him. That he thought of him as his own son, that he was his son. But he couldn't. He'd grown so accustomed to holding it all in that he knew no other way. So he said, You don't got to worry about that none. You just keep this between you and me and everythin will be alright. I got your back and you know that and I always will.

Gus looked up and almost cracked a smile, then closed his eyes. Tom left. Peeked around the house on his way out. Pile of empty beer cans in the kitchen. Trash can mounded over with refuse. Dust on the windowsills and the floor was filthy. Didn't linger, afraid that Rust would return. He went out the front door and down a side street to avoid crossing paths with Rust on the off chance that he did come driving into the subdivision. When he got to his truck, he sat there for a long time. The adrenaline waned. He was there until the windows had frosted over. He didn't feel sleepy, never once drifted off, but his body had never been so tired. His legs and back ached and he rolled his head on a swivel, trying to work out a kink that was stuck in there, attempting to elicit a relieving crack that never came.

Headlights on the county road pulled him from his thoughts. He watched in the distance. Thought he recognized Rust's truck. Let it get on up the street and he started his own truck and drove into the subdivision. A drive-by confirmed that Rust had returned; the off-white truck with a red horizontal stripe was parked cockeyed in the driveway. It was almost five thirty in the morning. It would begin to get light out before too long, and Tom sat in that predawn darkness in the cab of his truck with the heat running and thought of what he might do. Before he could figure it out though, Rust emerged from his house and got in the truck and backed out onto the street. He was alone. Gus must still be in the house. Tom thought about checking on the boy again but in a split second decided he needed to follow the boy's father. See what he was up to after a night seemingly without sleep. His anger had built through the ordeal and it drove him now, leaking as sweat from his pores. They pulled onto the highway. Tom followed at a distance, just far enough to avoid any suspicion, or that was his goal anyhow, and close enough to maintain a visual.

The truck pulled into town. Did not stop anywhere. Nowhere open to stop. Then it made a turn up a street and Tom followed it up that street until the street ran out of town and became another county road that would deadend at a winter trailhead where folks wanting to continue had to transfer to skis or snowmobiles. Some folks lived farther up in cabins and had snowmobiles parked there at the trailhead through the winter.

As they approached the trailhead, Tom eased off. Drove slower and slower, coming to a creep as he contemplated what he might do. He came to the final rise in the road and pulled off to the side. Cut the motor on the brown Dodge pickup and the white smoke billowing from the rusted pipe faltered in the frigid January air.

●

PART III

Marshal Tomlinson

I'd have to say this has been one of the longest winters of my life, though technically I suppose it's no longer winter. It can be hard to pinpoint the change in seasons in a place like this. Pretty ambiguous. Some springs hit hard and stay and the snow goes quick. Other times spring can feel like an extension of winter. Snowstorms into the middle of May. This year seems like somewhere in between. We're well into April now, late April even, and the days are warm and they's grass pokin out in town but the mountains keep gettin snow and it don't seem in no kind a hurry to melt off. Is what it is, I guess.

I stare out at the mountains, the snow, the woods, and nothin seems to change. On a day-to-day basis a whole lot has gone back to normal, or somethin resemblin it. Weird how that happens. Time knows nothin of the past. Just keeps marchin forward. So I know it'll come to an end eventually, but the waitin has been a torture on me.

Aint slept a whole lot. Never been what you might call

a good sleeper, I suppose. But it's gettin worse. Feelin run-down. All this worry and wonderin. Where we ever gonna find a solution to this mess? Could be one a those things that never lands. Just hangs out there in front a your face so you're always followin but can't never reach it. Not even goin nowhere, nowhere that matters anyhow. Can't get no rest from it. When I do sleep the dreams are somethin ter-rible. I just see the boy and the two men, Tom and Rust, and they're wanderin about in a fog. Not goin nowhere. Not runnin from nothin. Just aimless.

    I can't help but wonder on Tom. It's like I know he's still alive, cept I don't. It's a feelin. An ache in my gut. That's what's keepin me up, and I don't know which I'd prefer. Dead man lost out there in the woods or a killer on the loose. Can't quite bring myself to wish death on any man. I guess I'd hoped to find him, bring him to some sort of jus-tice, though I don't believe that would solve a thing. Aint a straightforward sort a matter. Everyone's dirty cept the boy, and he's been covered in stains by the sins of his father and his father's friend. I think I just want to know. For closure I guess. Though I know that odds are I won't get none. Still, a couple weeks from now, when the hills have melted out a bit, I think I'll take a drive up to the old Horak ranch. Check things out. Looked abandoned when we went in on snowmobiles earlier in the winter, but who knows. Gotta do somethin. Won't never get no rest if I don't.

Green

Here it was, the moment Green had both hoped for and dreaded through all the nights and days that Gus had been with him. Amelia Gomez, the woman from social services, was at the door and Gus was walking through the door and away from the house. Got into a car with the woman and drove away. Green watched the car drive down the street, disappear. Then he was standing there for God knows how long, as if something might be revealed to him through the simple act of remaining. Nothing came.

He wasn't sure why he felt the way he did. It was just a home visit to see if it could be a good permanent fit for Gus. He'd be gone for a few days and come home, but this wasn't Gus's home and to Green it felt like the real thing. A dry run for heartbreak.

He went back inside. Tried to go about his day.

They'd located Gus's family, or at least relatives. A

cousin of some kind. A woman who lived in a farming community northeast of Denver. Married without children. Green wished there had been other children wherever Gus ended up, but that was beyond his control. This would be good for the boy. The boy. This was for him. It had all been about him, and yet here was Green, the adult in the room, feeling sorry for himself.

The place felt empty and lonely, more so than it had been before Gus had come to live with him. He thought about that. The empty quiet had not bothered him before, or at least he had found a way over the years to not think about it. Now it was a blaring static that he had no way to quiet. He craved human interaction, and not just any but something deep, meaningful. Left the house. Began to walk into the heart of town then changed his mind and got in his car and drove. He didn't think about direction or where he might head. There were only so many places a car could take you in this county. He drove out the only highway headed the only direction the highway went, down valley, and he knew right away where he was headed when he got down there. Parked in front of the Home and went inside. Deb was behind the desk eating a sandwich and reading a magazine. She looked up as the bell announced the pastor's arrival. Gave him a discerning look.

What are you doing here? she asked.

It was a valid question. He only ever came here when he was doing his rounds and wasn't due for another week. It was unlike him to make unannounced visits to anywhere in his life.

I was just thinking about you and wondered if you had dinner plans this evening?

Her expression grew more discerning.

Are you asking me out on a date?

Maybe. I don't know. Like a dinner. Like a get-to-know-each-other kind of dinner. I'd just like to buy you dinner. Or that's the offer. If you want. No pressure.

His hands were sweating. That little voice of discernment began to speak up inside his head and it was wondering what the hell he thought he was doing.

Deb's demeanor shifted. She smiled. Laughed, a sort of lighthearted chuckle, and Green began to relax.

Sounds like a date, she said.

I guess so, said Green, abashed. But it doesn't have to be. It can be whatever.

But you want it to be a date.

Green said nothing. She had him pegged in a more outward, honest way than even he had himself pegged. Now he felt like he should have come in with more confidence. Not second-guessed himself, or not revealed that he was doing so.

I'd love to join you for dinner, she said before he could get another word in.

Ah, okay. Good. That's great. Um, what time do you like to eat?

Felt like more of an idiot. Eased up when she laughed again.

How about seven? Is that too late?

No. Not at all. Seven seems like a very appropriate time. How about the Brewery? I hear they have good burgers. Do you like burgers?

Love em. Seven it is.

Alright, I'll see you then.

Green stood there a moment longer, unsure how to end the interaction. Then simply said goodbye and left. Spent the afternoon running contrived errands to fill the time. A grocery list comprised from memory and a dawdling wander through the aisles of King Soopers. He went for a walk outside of town along the river. Sat and listened to the water moving. Evening came and he went to the Brewery a half hour early and ordered a beer and sat with his pad of paper and scribbled notes. Told himself he was working on that Sunday's sermon but when Deb walked in a few minutes after seven all he'd conjured were a few meaningless bullet points and a series of scratches where he'd crossed several things out. He set the paper and pen on the seat beside him and smiled up at Deb. A waiter came over before they could settle into conversation. She ordered a lager. He had the same. Said they'd need a minute on the food.

How you been? she asked after the waiter had gone.

Green was nervous. Good, he said. I've been well. How are you? Haven't seen you in a little while.

I know. I missed you last time you came in. Needed a personal day.

Yeah, I missed you too.

He immediately regretted that familiarity, realizing too late what she'd meant by the phrase as opposed to how it had fallen off his tongue. She made no indication that she either noticed or cared.

Everything alright? he asked.

Yeah. It's all good. I had to go visit my sister in Pueblo. She had some personal stuff going on.

Green didn't inquire as to the nature of the personal stuff.

I didn't know you had family in the state, he said.

And why would he? He knew very little of her outside of their professional interactions once every couple weeks.

Oh, they're all in the state, pretty much.

I didn't know that.

Yeah. I was a ranch kid, she said. Or at least that's how it started out. My family had a piece of land along the river off Highway 50. One of those little towns you've never heard of out east of Pueblo. It was hard times for my parents. I was pretty young. Can't say I remember all that much. Just little snippets. It was a beautiful spot. I remember that much. Then when the gas company came about and started putting wells on people's land, it was a hard thing for my parents to pass up. In the end they couldn't rationalize it, so they sold out and used the money they made to buy a place in town and open a small bakery. My mom had always wanted to do that. She kind of put her life on hold after marrying my dad. Raised us kids and kept the home while he ranched. Then with the bakery I guess they figured it was her turn. My siblings and I were old enough that we didn't need constant attention, so my dad helped my mom see her dream to fruition in any way that he could. I wouldn't call it a glamorous childhood, but it was a good one.

Is your whole family still out there?

Most of them. My folks are retired. One of my sisters ended up taking over the bakery, the one that's not in Pueblo. Then I have a brother up near Loveland. He works for his in-laws. They've got a feedlot or something related to that. Something with cattle. It smells awful up there. That's all I really know. He's quite a bit older than me and we were never all that close.

How about your sisters? You guys close?

Oh yeah. Especially the one in Pueblo. She's my best friend.

Here Deb paused and smiled, a little sheepish, Green thought, but in a playful kind of way.

How'd you end up here?

Dumb luck I guess. My mom said she always knew I'd be the one to leave home soon as I was old enough. I never disagreed with her. Just didn't want to give her the satisfaction of thinking she knew me better than I knew myself, which of course she did. I bounced around a little but I got my nursing degree from the college and just kinda fell into life here. It was easy.

A lull in the conversation. Their food arrived and they ate and chitchatted. Finished their beers.

What about you? Deb asked.

What about me?

What's your story?

Oh it's nothing special really. You already know about my parents. Their profession. My childhood was fairly uneventful. I grew up in a suburb of Grand Rapids. Got a degree in theology from Michigan State. Followed that with a master's and PhD program at a little school in Iowa. I had a teaching job as an adjunct faculty member there for a bit. I didn't enjoy it though, so after a while I took my parents' advice and did what I had to do to become a Lutheran pastor. Then I found this church that needed a pastor and here I am.

Their beers were empty. Half the patrons gone home or on to other places. Deb looked at the time on her phone.

Oh wow. It's already nine. I'd better get going. I have the early shift tomorrow.

Of course. Me too. Or, I have to get going. Not that I have the early shift. There is no shift for me really. Just service on Sundays and church functions.

She laughed. He felt clumsy.

This was really nice, she said.

Ya. It was.

On their way out, Deb seemed to remember something.

Hey. Do you like bingo?

Um. I guess, he said, not having any opinion on the game.

I mean I don't really. It's not something I usually do, but Tuesday bingo at the Elks is up to a $3,500 jackpot. Do you want to go?

Sure.

He still did not want to sound eager. Great, she said. It starts at six thirty.

Then, My friend Shelly might come.

Oh. Okay.

Was that a good thing? Being around her friends? He wasn't sure. Probably a good thing.

It'll be fun, she said.

She took his hand and squeezed his fingers and he was grateful that they had moved outside where it was darker, his face flushed with a boyish grin. Then she said, I'll see you Tuesday, and she crossed the street and disappeared into the night. Not until after she'd left did it cross his mind to offer her a ride, and he kicked himself for that and then felt relieved when he remembered his car was a mess.

The road was empty as he drove north on the highway. Headlights carved a narrow tunnel in the dark. Eyes of deer peered at him from the pastures, bodiless beacons, not seeing them until he came upon them and then a flash of brown on the fence line and they were gone. He put the groceries away and brushed his teeth. Lay in bed awake for hours with a pleasant buzz in his limbs, something he had not felt for a very long time.

Tom

Every day on the ranch grew warmer and the spring winds blew steady. The crust on the snow developed a red tinge of dust that accelerated the melting. Sagebrush extended farther skyward as the snow faded and rocks poked through, developing motes of bare ground around the bases. The house warmed during the day but still grew cold enough at night that Tom had burned through all of the scrap wood from the barn and started in on what was left of the tables and chairs in the house.

The road had melted out, still muddy, but it would be dry before long. His food had dwindled and he rationed accordingly. The hollow pain in his gut would go numb, returning not long after each meager meal. Fitful sleep came in short bursts and was plagued by unsettling dreams. Many of them contained visions of his mother. Occasionally his father. He would hear movement in the house, feel the presence of someone standing over him, paralyzed in a half sleep until he exploded into consciousness, thrashing his limbs and a forced cry, *Haaaa*, heart thumping. Then he'd rekindle a fire and sit cross-legged, lost in the embers until drowsiness returned.

At first he'd carried the ashes to the door and dumped them in the wind, the still-hot chunks of coals hissing in the snow, though now he'd lost all formality and what little ambition he may have had toward housekeeping. He eyed the walls with a curious hunger, every flammable substance turned to fuel in his mind. He wondered what it would take to tear up the floors, for that seemed to him the best option. Ample supply of wood while infringing as little as possible on the structural integrity of the building. Lately he'd begun piling the ash beside the tin, simply lifting one edge and letting the refuse slide to the floor. The boards beneath the sheet metal were blackened by the heat and the puff of ash settled across the room.

Then one night he judged to be sometime in late April or early May—it was hard to say, he left the confines of the house so infrequently that the passage of time had become difficult to gauge—he stoked the dwindling flames with a stack of posts from the railing along the stairs, the varnish burning off in an acrid black smoke that spiraled into the air. For a meal, he drained what was left of the syrup from the jar of peaches, savoring the liquid as it coated his throat and left a warm feeling in his belly, a feeling that persisted as he soon fell asleep and he was once again a younger man.

In the dream he was on the hillside above the hay meadow on his back and Rose's head rested on his chest. There was no speaking. Her face invisible to him and her hand scratching the hair below his naval. Circling. Searching. Lower. Then holding him. She was clothed only from the waist up and so was he. She was on him and her eyes were wet and she was telling him how much she loved him and he only wished she would not say that but she had and there was no taking it back because he knew that she meant it. The sun, setting, grew hot, and the warmth was on him, warmth from the sun and from the woman straddling him, at first pleasant, then growing until it burned and the hardness of the ground dug into him on the sharp points of his bones and he woke to an immense brightness and a roaring sensation. His eyes burned, breath sputtered. Everything was hot, too hot. Burning hot. The brightness of flame was unbearable and there came a crashing noise beside him. He rose and could not breathe. Ducked beneath the smoke. He ran, more of a shamble than anything else, eyes barely open. Heard a cracking sound beside his head and he dropped to his stomach in the kitchen doorway clutching at his shoulder where it had collided with the jamb. He pulled himself with the one good arm across the linoleum of the kitchen and knelt to open the door, falling into the fresh cold of outside. Smoke poured above him, rising into a clear black night filled with endless stars. He remembered the rifle with a jolt of panic and without thinking he scrambled back into the building, embers flying as expanding air burst the wood from its grain. The air was hot and rancid with smoke, every breath a scraping, searing pain. He fell to the floor and did a combination crawl-slither beneath the ceiling of smoke. His eyes watered and his vision was blurred. He made it back out with the rifle that was somehow not burnt though the barrel was hot enough that it hurt when he touched it.

Tom sat on the ground and leaned against the exterior wall of the barn. Watched flames leap from the roof of the house, vanish in the night. Cool air was like fresh water in his lungs. He drank it down in gulps. Heard the popping and roaring and crashing of the fire. Felt the awareness of different sensations come into his body. The cold and wet on his back. Wetness everywhere, a massive sweat initiated by both heat and adrenaline.

His breathing subsided, heart rate slowed to a steady thrum. The night was cold but the heat from the fire was immense and he sat for a long time and watched his world burn. The ghosts and memories, of things that had happened in that house, gone up in a raging ball of flame. He wasn't sure about the ghosts and did not believe the memories would ever go away, or not the feelings from them, not at this point in his life, yet there was an unburdening sense of relief in the absurdity of complete destruction. Smoke pouring skyward was weight siphoned from his mind. Maybe it was like a chain being broken, the heavy ball it tethered left to rust. Not gone but he was no longer within its clutch. His eyelids grew heavy and he fell asleep. Woke when a crack broke the night and he opened his eyes in time to see a portion of the roof cave in, the walls begin to buckle. As the sun rose, the building had been reduced to rubble, smoldering embers, a few blackened studs reaching like bony fingers from the crushed-rock foundation. The stone chimney stood alone like some monument to a past life. Even in the absence of flames he could still feel the heat from the pile and he dozed in the rising sun until he woke and there was a breeze that had cooled him. Black ash flew from the remnants of the house, a moribund confetti scattered across the yard.

Tom rose and went into the barn. In the storage room he found an old saddle blanket, and he spread it on the loose hay and wrapped himself in it and slept. The sun was high, beating down on the yard when he woke. The smell of burnt wood and other, more acrid things perfumed the air. His gut ached with hunger. What little food stores were left had vanished in the fire. He walked the yard and surveyed the rubble. Nothing to see. He looked at the sky, the hills. The valley below where the hay meadow was almost bare of snow. Back in the barn he rummaged around to see what he might find. Picked up a handful of hay and put some in his mouth, chewed it and let it fall from his lips. Spent a few minutes picking brittle strands from his teeth while his gums bled. Took a loose chunk of leather from a torn piece of tack and stuck it in his mouth. Bitter taste of dirt and oil. Hard as metal. He left it there and sucked on it. After a while it softened and he gnawed on it until his jaw grew sore. Stuck it in his pocket. Searched every corner of the barn, even digging through the eons' worth of chaff. In the corner of a stable beneath a pile of rubber feed pans there was an old aluminum trash can and he removed the lid and found it half full of grain, maybe oats or barley, that would have been a treat for the horses. He dipped a hand and pulled a load of grain out, the kernels falling off his skin like water. Much of the grain had either deteriorated or been eaten by insects, the cores of the kernels gone to dust and naught left but translucent husks, though there remained a decent amount of actual grain. He popped a few in his mouth and chewed. They were hard but not inedible, and between the kernels were the dried-up carcasses of some kind of worm or maggot. *Good,* he thought, *carbs* and *a little protein.* He looked closer and determined that the mice had not gotten into it, which was a good thing. Probably the only reason there was any left. He threw a few more into his mouth and sucked on them a little before biting and the hard kernels turned to a faintly sweet mush that stuck in his teeth.

Tom stayed in the barn and thought of spring, the drying road. Implications to the broader world. He'd been sheltered by winter and the snow and now the hills were becoming accessible. No one lived here, that was true, but he was not sure that no one would come up and check the place out once they were able to drive. It had already crossed his mind on numerous occasions that his truck had been left at the scene of the murder and that two and two would in all likelihood have been put together months ago, probably the same day they found the body. It wasn't that he worried much about being caught or facing judgment. Hell, a large part of him did not care whether he lived or died. But there were things he wanted to do before he lost his freedom. More than anything he longed to check on the boy, though he could not figure a way that it would be possible, given that he had no idea where the boy was, and even if he did, how would he get close? The night prowling had worked before because no one had been paying attention, and he at least had a home base he could go back to. Now all of that was gone. The one thing in his favor was that he figured most folks had already written him off for dead. He thought that might give him some leeway. More and more though, a return to civilization seemed inevitable.

On an afternoon while rummaging the barn's contents, Tom came across an old mirror that was pocked by blemishes and a brief moment of confusion struck him as he did not recognize the face that stared back at him. Wiped the surface with the grimy sleeve of his shirt and accepted that the mirror was not lying, the image clear enough. Ragged beard and baggy cheeks hung off the bone of his face.

There was gray in his beard, far more than he remembered there ever being, and his hair was wild and rat-nested, half dreadlocked like a mangy dog and also gray, more so at the roots. He stared at himself. Lost track of time and looked around from his vantage in the barn loft as if coming to, everything a daze. In another barn ramble he found a pair of scissors, ancient and heavy, though sharp enough, and he sat in front of the mirror and sheared the wiry hair from his face. Through slow progress, layers peeled, he began to see the man that he recognized, if a little withered. When he'd cropped his facial hair down as close as he could get it, he carried on with the hair on his head, lopping off strands and chunks and bringing it down to a rough short cut. When he'd finished, he admired himself in the mirror. Though he looked more like himself, he still did not feel that it was the same man staring back at him as it would have been only a few months ago, but he at least recognized the features of his own face. He set the scissors on the floor of the loft and went back down to ground level. Stared at the claw-footed tub. Then he acted. Grabbed it by the rim and dragged it through the hay and out the door of the barn. It was heavy and he took a number of breaks, sat on the rim of the tub to rest. Kept dragging. When he'd reached a spot in the yard sufficiently far from the barn, he stopped. Found a few pieces of broken cinder block and propped up the spot with the missing foot. Went back in the barn and gathered as much loose wood as he could find. An old pallet and a stack of boards. He piled them next to the tub. The next part took some doing. After some searching about he found an old five-gallon bucket with the handle broken off and he used it to shuttle loads of water from the well tap behind the barn, taking frequent breaks. It was a long process and it was evening before the tub had been filled. He set to kindling a fire. Still had a few matches from the cabin and got some flames going, fed them with the ends of boards, sliding them closer as they burned down and soon the orange flame climbed up the sides of the of the tub and blackened the ceramic coating. Watched a sliver of sickled moon rise over the hills to the east and fed the flames. He dipped a finger into the water to test the heat, and sometime after the moon had risen, enough time that a fair bit of sky separated it from the horizon, the water became too hot to touch. Tom let the fire die and after some waiting stripped down to nothing and began the process of entering the water, the temperature nearly too hot but not quite. Fully submerged, he lay back, dunked his head and stayed with his face exposed, ears beneath the surface, and stared at the sky. Before the water cooled he took a broken chunk of sandstone he'd found in the rock foundation of the house and rubbed it everywhere on his body. It was too dark to see the water or how grimy it might have been, but he could smell the odor that rose from its surface, gamy and oily. After he'd scrubbed himself he lay in the water until it grew cold and then climbed out of the tub and stumbled back to the barn. Wrapped himself in the blanket and lay on the hay until he fell asleep, dreaming of warmth.

Days ticked by. Tom counted time's passing with the vanishing of snow. It was all but gone from the ranch yard, only a few glaciated piles on the north sides of buildings where roofs had shed in the winter. The road had dried, or appeared to have. He had not walked down to look, but it seemed that the gravel had softened in color where he could see it and most of the ground around the ranch yard had gone dry as well.

Tom had walked up the hill above the house, or above the spot where the house had stood, and lay on the ground surveying the land. Let his mind wander. Thought about what it would be like to live here again, get the ranch working. Get some hay growing. Maybe a few animals. He was curious what the ditches were like. Odds were they would be so choked with dead grass that quite a bit of work would need to be done in order to get the water flowing. The fences were useless, he'd seen that on his way in, the wire slack or on the ground, T-posts rusted through at ground level and the wooden H-braces all but rotted away. That alone was a full season's worth of work for one person. And the house was gone. Didn't matter, though. It was all a daydream, even he knew it would never happen. He'd gone too far down this side road of life for that. Still, he imagined. Stared out at the sky, spotted a speck of black that moved and grew and came closer and he saw that it was some kind of bird, perhaps a hawk or eagle. Maybe a raven. No. A hawk. He watched it hover and rise, then take a swooping dive, turn and climb again. Held steady in an updraft. He closed his eyes and thought about what it would be like to fly, and when he opened his eyes and looked down at the pasture and the road, something there caught his attention. A trail of dust rose from the lower road and drifted off over the pasture. The dust cloud moved along the road behind what appeared to be a vehicle. Tom watched this new development for only a moment before the panic struck and he jumped up and ran back to the barn.

The first and only thing he went for was the rifle. It was leaned up against the wall beside the door to the tack room. He slung the shoulder strap over his neck and went out the back of the barn. He'd only have a couple more minutes at best before the car pulled into the yard. He thought for a moment of running off into the hills, but it was a long way before the land or trees provided any visual cover and the low hum of a motor came through the air before he had made up his mind to move, so he stayed put. So long as the driver stopped in the logical center of the yard, he'd be alright, for a minute anyway. He still didn't know who this was or what they might be up to. What, if anything, they would be looking for, or whom, though he thought he could give an educated guess.

Gravel crunched and the motor slowed and was killed.

Heard a door open, a dinging sound proclaiming to the world that the keys were still in the ignition or perhaps the lights on. The door shut before the dinging stopped so he figured it was keys in the ignition. He thought they would have turned the lights off if that were the case. Then there was silence. The light breeze all but inaudible off the loose tin on the barn's roof. Then footsteps growing quieter with each passing stride. They were walking away from him. Up to the house.

Tom ventured a few slow steps to the corner of the barn. Poked his head around. Saw the white-and-brown SUV with a red-and-blue plastic bar on the roof and a door panel plastered in big letters reading MARSHAL. Ducked back around the barn and cursed under his breath. He was running on adrenaline, not thinking. All action. He figured his best move would be to wait in the barn. Anyone wanting to look about the ranch would find their way in there eventually. The door was open and, once inside, it would not take a whole lot of deduction to figure out that someone had been about the place. So Tom went in the back way and found a spot to hide near the front where he hoped he would not be noticed. Then he waited.

●

The marshal had taken the drive on a whim. The case was not so much cold as it was dead. What everyone told him.

What he believed, though there must have been a part of him that still hoped, otherwise why would he have taken this drive? What would there be to see on a ranch that had not been inhabited in about a decade?

The idea had come a while back but cemented after he visited Tom Horak Sr. in the assisted living facility. He knew the man's state. Knew that nothing would come of it, but he still wanted to go there and see for himself. And he saw. Saw a man at the end of his life, perhaps unaware of his current state. Like a living purgatory. The oxygen tank only prolonged that state. No one there with the authority to pull the plug. Though would they have? Would he if it had been his father? He thought that he would. It was a quality-of-life thing. Hard to say without truly being faced with it.

He removed his hat. Stood there for a few minutes. Then left. Thanked the woman who was on duty and drove out of town.

The deputy had wanted to come, he said for backup. Backup for what? he'd asked and had gotten a blank stare in response.

It was a pleasant drive. Even if he found nothing, that alone made it worth the trip. Though he also thought the peace of mind of having checked would be a good thing for him. Anything else was a bonus.

The road had that look of having had little to no traffic in Lord knew how many years. Weeds grew up the center.

Parallel lines of bare gravel where generations of wheels and tires had rolled and compacted the dirt and road base so that nothing could grow there. Dust trailed off behind him. Amazing how quick things could dry out in this country. Pulled into the ranch proper and parked in no spot in particular. Just a general central location. Sat there in the cab for a minute, his legs heavy from the drive. Left the keys there in the ignition, a habit of his, maybe a bad one, but it was a small town and he wasn't even in town right now.

The first thing he noticed was the river rock hearth that appeared to be growing out of a pile of burnt rubble where he knew from his previous visit the house should have been standing. Walked up to take a look. The marshal could smell the faint odor of charcoal and wondered how long that smell would stick around after a fire. Something like a tingle at the back of his neck. He noticed it. The vacant feeling the ranch had when he'd arrived had vanished, and though he did not think he was in any danger of firing his gun, his trigger hand, relaxed, hung at his side not far from the holster. He walked around the perimeter, kicked at a few blackened boards that had held their shape. Thought about walking through and seeing if there was anything worth looking at but didn't want to track all that soot back into the vehicle. He supposed someone would have to root around in there, but he'd tackle that problem when he got back to town. Turned his attention to the barn. Body tensed for a reason he could not put his finger on.

●

The barn had been the first structure to be built on the ranch in the days before anyone lived there. An outpost of a large-scale ranching operation of the late nineteenth century, its original purpose was much as it had been throughout its history, and that was to store hay and equipment. Over the years, certain things wore down. The roof had been reworked three times in its life and only leaked a little, the workers not even bothering to remove the old tin, just layering it on like a flimsy metal cake. Some of the siding had been replaced on the back after a hard winter when overhanging ice from the roof had swung in and punched a hole. At some point the loft and storage room were added and the doors were updated. Other than that, though, not much had changed. The bones of the place were what they had always been and so the scene that played out could have been taken from something out of the old West. The marshal, sure he drove a motor vehicle as opposed to a horse, was like any other lawman in the long history of lawmen in that part of the country. Wore a hat and a badge and carried a pistol on his hip, the big iron, though his was a modern spin on the stereotype, made of some alloy so it weighed less and it was smaller than the six-shooters most kids playing cowboys and Indians would have imagined themselves to be carrying.

Tom had been hiding off to the side of the front door just inside in a darker section of shadow. He heard the marshal's footsteps getting louder as he approached, stepped inside, and stood in the light of the doorway and looked up. Tom waited. Watched the marshal out the corner of his eye and tried not to breathe. Then the marshal took two steps, and at the same moment that Tom lunged forward and brought his leg up, the dried-out, bone-hard sole of his bootheel making contact with the marshal's ribs, he fired off a shot from the Model 70 hunting rifle and put a hole through every roof that barn had ever known. The marshal did not see the hole but he heard the shot and felt a crack in his side as he collapsed forward, struggling to breathe. Tom fell on top of him and put the rifle crosswise on the back of his neck.

Tom realized it was the same position he'd had Rust in when last he'd seen him, and he let up a little. The man beneath him could breathe but was still restrained.

Arms up, you bastard. Put your hands up above your head or you're gonna die.

The marshal grunted and wheezed. Peeled his hands from the awkward position he'd landed in and lay them out above his torso. His stiff shoulders would not allow him to stick them straight up, so they flopped out at a cartoonish angle that caused him quite a bit of pain.

Tom squirmed around and got his legs over the rifle and freed up a hand that he used to fish around at the marshal's waist. After some fumbling he found the holster. Snapped it open and slid the pistol out. Stuck it in his back pocket.

Alright now, said Tom.

The marshal still had not said a word. Tom eased off and stood. Pressed the tip of the rifle barrel into the marshal's back.

Alright now. Stand up.

The marshal pushed up, the pang in his ribs like a knife in his side. The initial adrenaline had begun to wane, the jolt that had come from believing he'd been shot. He wasn't sure where the bullet had gone but he was confident it had not struck his body. It crossed his mind to try to reason with this person, but the wind was still half knocked out of him and he couldn't manage more than a groan.

Now walk, Tom said. That door over there, that's where you're headed.

They made their way across the chaff-scattered barn floor toward the storage room. As they approached, Tom's pulse quickened. The marshal stepped up into the room and Tom gave him a push and he fell headlong onto the floor as Tom slammed the door behind him and took the key from his pocket and turned the dead bolt. Then he wasted no time. Went to the vehicle outside. Saw the key that he'd prayed to find there, turned the ignition, and drove out down the road. He wasn't sure where he would go until he began to drive but as soon as the wheels began to turn, he knew exactly where he was headed.

Marshal Tomlinson

A place like this sometimes you feel like you're tryin to *keep the rest of the world out. You watch the national news and it's nothin but sensationalized hoopla about nonsense interspersed with gruesome murders and our nation's latest conquests overseas. One conflict after another, but it's all really the same thing, even though I can't say exactly what that is. Greed maybe. Power mongering. Different names for the same sin. No real substance but fear. People got to have somethin to fear now that God's gone by the wayside.*

To me it seems like people these days have got this energy buildin in them and if they don't find some outlet they just snap. As if for four or five generations our country's been workin its ass off toward some unobtainable goal we call progress, happiness, industrialization, the future, enlightenment. Whatever. It's like wanderin around in a fog trying to snatch up the wind. And I'm not sure we can do it for much longer before somethin breaks. We forget that things weren't always this way. Not so long ago life was simpler. You think how much the world has changed in the last hundred years, hundred and fifty years, compared to the eons before that. The jump is unfathomable when you really sit down and consider it. Don't get me wrong. We've had some great things come out of this. Modern medicine. Centralized government. Electricity. Advancements in mental health care. Better education. Gender equality, to an extent, more'n there used to be anyhow. And so on down the line. But there are side effects to the way we've gained those things. It reminds me of those graphs we used to look at in math class where there was a curve that swooped up against a line, comin infinitely close to that line yet never touchin it, and as it did, it would skyrocket into infinity. Mathematicians have spent lifetimes studyin, just tryin to understand what happens to that line the closer it gets to this place that it will never touch. A destination to which it will never arrive but will always be gettin closer. That's what I think is happenin inside of people today. What happens to a society as that energy skyrockets and we come closer and closer to somethin we will never obtain? What happens when people realize they will never achieve their dreams because their dreams are based on some utopian lie ingrained in them since childhood? Where is the tippin point, and what lies on the other side?

We all have that tippin point. Probly some sort of collective tippin point. Families. Groups of people. Anyone with any kind of shared history. Hell. All of humanity.

Scares the hell out of me. The things we are capable of when pushed to the limit.

Tom

•

AFTER HIS MOTHER'S FUNERAL, TOM DROVE OUT TO the ranch to see his father. The two hadn't spoken at the service, hadn't spoken in years. Tom hadn't thought about how long it had been since he'd last come out to see his parents until his mom was dead and he suddenly longed to see her.

He found his dad in the barn. So much older than he remembered him. A hump in his back below the neck. Hair lacking most of its former color. Balding on top. He wore grease-lacquered coveralls torn halfway to the knee on one leg, cuffs bunched above his boots as if he'd just slipped them on, neither pulling over nor tucking in the pant legs.

Early winter. Temperature hovered in the mid-teens.

Inside the barn their breath rose in bursts of white steam that dissipated in the low yellow light. The old man broke flakes of hay. Tossed them into a pen where a muscled brown steer dropped its head. Came up with a tuft of hay undulating in the corner of its mouth as the lower jaw slid from side to side with its chewing.

Tom Sr. looked over his shoulder. Hey, he said, and turned back to watch the steer.

Hey, said Tom.

Tom leaned against the slats on the pen, rough-cut lumber smoothed by the rubbings of countless inhabitants. Bits of fur in the splintered grain.

So, the old man said, not looking at his son, eyes on the animal. How are things?

Tom brushed the curve of the steer's horn with the backs of his knuckles. Things are good, he said. Or, you know. Good as they can be.

His dad pulled another flake apart and scattered it on the far side of the pen. The steer grunted and moved to the new hay, stepping on what it had been eating in the process.

How are you holdin up? Tom asked.

Oh. His face tightened. Good as can be expected.

After a moment, Your mother would've liked to see you more.

Tom took a deep breath.

She didn't talk about it much, but I know it was always a disappointment to her.

Tom shifted his weight from one foot to the other and back again. Dug a thumbnail into the soft wood of the fence. I'm sorry I've been a disappointment.

Well, that's not what I said.

Same difference.

A long quiet. Crunch-grind of the masticating steer.

I know it wasn't always easy for you growin up. I know that a big part of that was me.

Tom said nothing. A short, bitter laugh.

I don't think your mom deserved what she got.

Oh yeah? What did she get?

Maybe if you'd come around more you'd be able to answer that question yourself. I guess that's kinda the point.

Well, she can blame you for that one.

You wanna hold a grudge for the rest of your life, that's your call.

Maybe.

You know I quit drinkin when your mom took sick. Bit of an eye-opener for me.

It was true. The near-ubiquitous flask had not made an appearance in some time. Tom could not see past it.

Toward the end there, I was all she had. Same goes for me to her. We talked about things. Hashed out a lot a shit.

Mm-hmm.

She forgave me a lot of the things that happened. Said so anyhow. I don't know. Maybe you never will.

Tom stared at the steer.

I just don't know why you ever held anything against her. No words. He listened. Anger rising.

I hope at least for your sake you can find a way to forgive her. I don't know why you never came around when she needed it. I guess that's your business. I know I'm a big part of that. I guess I just wanted to say I'm sorry. For everything.

Tom could not find words. The seething had overtaken him. He could not look at his father, who simply patted him on the back and walked away. *Sorry. For everything.* It struck Tom that his father had not been specific about what everything entailed. Not that it would have made any difference. Tom was beyond forgiveness. *Everything* could not be undone. He listened to the chuff of his father's boots as he crossed the yard and heard the door to the kitchen opening and shutting. He stood watching the steer that faced away from him. Scratched at its flank and it switched its tail. The last piece of livestock left on the place, kept almost as a pet, something to keep his father busy, keep him company. Docile old men past their primes. Killing time. He threw it a few more flakes of hay and walked out into the late-evening light.

The windows in the house glowed with warmth. He could see his father through the window and the old feelings rose again. Frustration. Balled-up anger. Everything his father had said through the years. All the shit he'd done. To Tom. The hell he'd put his son through. For what? Some arbitrary grasp at control? Tom was still angry, but his father, it seemed, no longer reciprocated that antagonism. Something about his mother's decline had softened Tom Sr. Tom, the boy, Tommy, held it. A last gasp of old habits, unwilling to drown. He gritted his teeth and drove home without saying goodbye.

Six months later he helped his father move off the ranch and into an assisted living facility in Bonfisk. Two months after that he received a letter from the man. Tore open the envelope. Read and reread the words. Set it on the counter with the other mail. Bills and junk, some of it opened, some not. It stayed there until one of his manic cleaning sessions when he threw everything away. He picked it up, looked at the paper in his hands, dug the old cigar box out from under his bed, folded the letter, and placed it there with the feathers and stones.

A couple years passed. Sometimes when he thought of his father he felt like driving out that way. Just to see him, what had become of him. He was down on that end of the valley enough that it wouldn't take much to just swing by for a visit. Just couldn't ever bring himself to do it. Wasn't even sure why his father had gone there in the first place. What sort of state his mind and body were in. There hadn't been any correspondence since the letter, and he let the impulse slide to the back of his mind.

Time, he thought. There would always be time. Always passing. Moment to moment. Until one day time would run out. Then maybe it wouldn't matter anymore.

●

Time had come and gone and finally it had run out. Tom took a roll of duct tape from the glove compartment and left the marshal's car on a vacant side road outside of town and walked through the sage hills to the edge of houses. A rise that overlooked the community. He sat there and waited for dark to fall. When it had, he rose and walked the streets. He'd been in this town countless times in his life but walking through now it felt like entering a foreign land. Everything was new and held a sort of clarity for him. The light of the thin moon through budding leaves in the cottonwoods. A front porch with a couch and grill and two children's bicycles in the yard. A quiet night. A couple cars passed by. Tom kept to the shadows and tried to hide the rifle with the length of his body.

He knew the general location of the old folks' home where his father was, or where he used to be, hoped he was still there, though he had circled a few different blocks until he saw a sign on a grass lawn before a squat building that read COTTONWOOD ESTATES: ASSISTED LIVING FACILITY. He stood on the lawn. There were lights on inside. The main room in the center with unshaded windows showed a lamp beside a couch and more light coming from a place out of sight. Other windows up and down the length of the building with shades drawn either dark or with filtered light. He walked to the front door and stepped inside the building.

Deb

Deb was tired. It had been a long day, but she had gained a little steam as her shift dwindled toward quitting time. She was working late, had covered for Doren, who would cover for her in the morning so she could sleep in. A fair trade-off in her book. That wasn't what had kept her going though. It was the prospect of what was to come when she got off from her shift. She had a date, like, a real date. She and the preacher man, as she called him only to herself, had gotten dinner that one night, but she had not considered that a date, though she knew that he had. She was leery of dating, a side effect of being single into her upper thirties. The hardening brought on by years was real. But she had softened, or this man who was quite a bit older than she was had begun to soften her. Or she was just softening around him. It was difficult to pinpoint, but when it came down to it that didn't matter. She was going with the flow.

Her shift wound down. She had gone through the checklist at the end of her normal shift and was able to spend this extra time getting ready for her date. Had changed her clothes and cleaned herself up a little. Didn't take much time. Deb had never been very high-maintenance. Then she sat in the office chair and waited. Read a magazine. *Better Homes & Gardens.* Not really reading, looking at photographs, skimmed a few things here and there. Had almost fallen asleep when the bell on the front door jingled. She looked at the clock. Doren wasn't due for another half hour. She stood up and stepped out of the office.

Green

Green had gotten out of the shower at 5:00 p.m. There were still hours left before Deb was supposed to arrive. She was on night shift, or evening shift. Working late. She had insisted on driving to him that evening. Said it was her turn. Green had relented. Gus was still away on his home visit, had been for nearly a week, and so Green had suggested she come to his place. He'd cook, or attempt to. Years of living alone had narrowed his palate, but having Gus around had begun to awaken that bit of creativity in him. He was baking a whole chicken. Some potatoes in the oven with it and sautéed asparagus with garlic, salt, and pepper. A good Midwestern meal, something his mother would have made. Deb wasn't from the Midwest but she seemed hearty in that way, in the way that the women in his early life had been. One of the things he liked best about her, touching some familiarity in his subconscious. He'd timed it so the bird would be in

the oven when Deb arrived, or said she was going to. The
house would smell great. Everything would be great. He
told himself that. Danced around the kitchen feeling the
best he had in years.

Tom

The bell sounded as Tom pushed the front door open and he stepped into the room and saw a woman appear from a door behind a desk. He hadn't anticipated her, hadn't anticipated anything. There was no real plan, only a destination. Not sure how he'd get there or what he would do when he did, just pushed forward through improvisation. Raised the rifle and pointed it in the woman's general direction. He didn't think of aiming. The rifle was not loaded. He'd seen to that. Didn't want any accidents. It was for show, and judging by the look on the woman's face, the show did not disappoint. Even before he said anything she put her hands in the air. Tremors throughout her body.

That's good, ma'am, he said. You don't want no trouble and neither do I.

Tom craned his neck to look into the office. The woman stood there with her arms above her head, lowering them a bit as they grew tired.

There anyone else here?

She looked at him and nodded.

Not the old people, he said. Anyone else workin?

Shook her head.

Okay, good. Now you just go on back in that office and sit down. Don't touch anythin. I'm gonna follow you. I'm watchin you, so don't try nothin.

The woman did as she was told. She went slow, which Tom appreciated. Sat in the chair and he pulled on the end of the roll of duct tape he'd taken from the marshal's SUV and wrapped it around her arms on the armrests down to and including the tops of her hands. He stuck the corner of a five-inch strip to the edge of the desk and used the rest to strap her torso to the back of the chair and a few wraps around her legs for good measure. Stood back and looked at her. She stared at him. He could see fear and some confusion on her face.

Okay then. Where's Thomas Horak at?

Blinked. Stuttered. What?

Thomas Horak. Tom Horak Sr. Where's his room? Is he still here?

Ye-yes. But.

Sht. I don't want nothin else from you. You just tell me where he's at and I'll figure the rest out.

She stared at him. Seemed to be examining him. Contemplating something.

Any day now, lady.

Down the hall on your right. Third door on the left. His name is on a placard beside the door.

Tom relaxed. Thank you, he said. Now I'm gonna leave you here. I don't think there's much to get you into trouble, but just in case.

Tom took the five-inch strip from the edge of the desk and moved toward her face. She recoiled and turned her head.

Now, now, he said. This is just a precautionary thing. It'll hurt when they pull it off, but other than that there won't be no harm done. I just need you to cooperate, so don't try and bite me or nothin. You may not believe this but I have never struck a woman and I do not intend to, but I do have some business to attend to here this evenin, and I will attend to it one way or another.

She stared. He moved toward her and she held steady.

One last thing, Tom said. Where's the keys? I need to lock the doors. This won't take long but I don't want to be interrupted.

The woman hesitated. Nodded to the space behind Tom. Top center drawer of the desk. There's a door at the end of each hallway and the front makes three. That's all there is.

Tom smiled. See, he said. We can be, well, maybe not friends, but we can be friendly. Still . . .

He stuck the duct tape across her lips and pressed it into her skin, taking care to pull her hair behind her ears so it would not catch in the tape. He could hear her breathing through her nose. Left her there without another word.

The keys were where she said they'd be. He took them and first locked the front door then went to the ones at the ends of the hallways. He did a search and found no other entrances. Then passed the front desk, glanced at the woman who stared right back, and entered the hallway. Stopped at the door that bore his father's name. His name. Turned the handle and pushed.

Green

The timer on the oven sounded and Green pulled the bird out and set it on the stove to rest. Set the timer again. Deb was late. That was alright. He'd hoped she would call but maybe something had happened there and she was busy. Then his mind wandered. What if something had happened on the drive? An accident. Odds were against it. Probably she was just late and hadn't called to let him know. This seemed out of character, but then he told himself that he didn't know her all that well. What was really in or out of character for her? Began to question everything. Even his good mood and the chicken. Maybe he was living in a fantasy world where everything he thought was happening between them was limited to the space between his ears. The timer beeped. And beeped. And beeped. After a bit he rose and turned it off. Went to the window and stood looking down the street. At last he got a hold of himself. There was at least one thing left in his power to do. He picked up the phone.

Deb

Deb sat strapped to the chair. She could not see a clock and had no way of knowing how much time had passed until she heard the rattle of the front door. A pause and another rattle as someone tried to push it open. She did not know whether Doren had a key or not, but when she heard nothing more from the front door she figured he must not. He was likely checking the other doors around the building. Things were silent for a time. Her mind raced and wandered, had been since she was left there. She had not come up with any ideas. There was more rattling and more silence followed. A long period of silence. The phone rang. It was right there in front of her on the desk, the red light glowing to announce the incoming call, as if the ringing were not enough. The ringing stopped. A minute later the red light began blinking to let her know a voicemail had been left. She sat. A while later the phone rang again. Stared at the receiver until the ringing stopped. Nothing she could do but wait.

Tom

Tom walked into a dark room and stood. Heard the mechanical *tick-hiss* of the oxygen. Beside a table in a corner was a stand-alone lamp and he pulled a metal segmented chord and let his eyes adjust to the light. Turned around and looked at his father in the bed. Went to the bedside and stood over him. Put his hand on his brow, a forearm resting atop the pillow. Sat in a chair beside the lamp.

Tom beneath the lamp slumped in the chair with the rifle between his legs. The remainder of the room lay in gradients of half-scrimmed shadow and an orangey light. Took a deep breath and stared at his father. The man was not dead. The rise and fall of his chest was too apparent for that. And yet, he was not exactly living. Tom thought about that. Wondered what might be going on in his father's mind. Perhaps nothing. Endless conversing with God. Would he know that he was living or dead? Would he have any recollection of his life? The life-flashing-before-your-eyes phenomenon was supposed to be real, but how Tom understood it, that was more of a veering-into-oncoming-traffic sort of thing where everything hits all at once like a water balloon plastered across the windshield. Maybe what his father was experiencing was something more akin to a slow dissection. Would the memories evoke any sort of emotion? Tom hoped there were certain things his father regretted. Things from Tom's upbringing. He thought about forgiveness. Did he forgive his father for the things he'd put him and his mother through? That was a good question. He felt sorry for the man. Didn't think anyone should be held in this state of limbo. Tom was the next of kin, and if anyone had the authority to pull the plug, so to speak, it would be him, though he held no illusions of anyone giving him that power. It occurred to him that should he forgive his father, the man would be unable to receive that forgiveness. Not that that was an option for him. But still, who then would it be for?

He looked at the vinyl tube coming off his father's face. Wondered how long it would take. If he just cut that cord. Would it be like drowning in air? Tom shuddered at the thought. Then anger tensed his body, rage building inside. He clutched at the cold barrel of the rifle leaned against the inside of his thigh. Went back to that place.

An image of fire and lead exploding out of iron pressed against the side of his skull. Closed his eyes and tweaked his head to the side so hard his neck spasmed. Tears leaked out the inside corners of his eyes. He leaned over and put his mouth over the end of the barrel and stayed that way, the metallic taste and a ringing in his teeth. Rose and leaned back in the chair with the rifle across his lap. Let out a gasp.

Tom closed his eyes for a while. He wasn't tired. No desire to sleep. He opened his eyes and looked out the window beside him. Peeled the drapes back to look at the darkened street, a solitary streetlamp like something out of an old movie. Returned to the room and looked at his father. Felt something like pity. He stood and went to him. Put his hand on the man's neck. Felt the faint pulse there. Pressed his hand against the windpipe, harder. Watched the involuntary opening of the jaw, the muscles reacting, a body struggling to live. It amazed Tom, the will to live, even in this state. To his surprise Tom teared up. Released the grip on his father's throat and, with it, a bit of the poisonous energy he'd been drinking for so many years. What was the point of vitriol when the recipient of it was not there to take it? The feeling did not vanish but shifted, dissipated a little and turned further inward. It was all on him now. No one to blame but himself.

Tom heard a motor and looked out at a police cruiser

passing on the street. He knew there would be a limited amount of time here. Seemed appropriate. Thought about anything else he might want to say. Nothing came. He sat in the chair, leaned back, and waited for the end.

Epilogue

Green and Deb drove out of town on an afternoon in early autumn after Deb got off work. It was Friday. A weekend trip. They'd been looking forward to this road trip for some time. Green was going to meet her family. She'd told them about him not long after they began dating in earnest. Her sister had known who he was in the early days. They had that kind of relationship, the sisters. Sharing secrets and dreams and things no one else knows. Before that, though, she and Green had another destination.

They passed through Denver and stayed in a hotel downtown. It cost more than either of them would consider spending under normal circumstances, but the trip was a celebration of sorts. The two settling into something. Ate at a Brazilian steakhouse off the Sixteenth Street mall and slept in the next day, staying in bed through mid-morning. Ordered room service breakfast and got a late checkout.

They drove north out of the city and took an exit off the interstate up past Fort Lupton and headed east onto the plains. Twenty-some-odd miles out they turned right on a bullet-straight gravel road. Sign said COUNTY ROAD 8H. They drove through fields of corn and wheat already harvested and the leftover plant cut down and tilled into the soil for the spring. Long stretches of fallow land and barren prairie. White-tailed deer grazed here and there, unperturbed by the passing vehicle.

I think this is it, said Deb as they approached a narrow road on the left with a mailbox atop a post at the end.

Green turned his Subaru onto the drive and another half mile down they came to an old farmhouse with a latticed porch shaded by a viny plant. Deb thought maybe they were grapes. As they stepped out of the car a woman appeared through the front door.

You must be Morris and Deborah, she said as they approached the house.

And you must be Polly, said Green.

They shook hands and sat on wicker chairs beneath the vines. Waited as Polly fetched a pitcher of ice water, sprigs of mint suspended in sweating glasses, and sat across from the couple.

Gus is out with Forest. My husband. They should be along anytime. They went out lookin for deer. Huntin season's comin up.

Green let the ice tinkle in his glass, watched the condensation trickle down onto his hand. You're a cousin of the boy's father, he said. Not really a question, just filling the space.

Yes. His ma and my pa were brother and sister. They've all passed on, sadly. Not a particularly healthy bunch. They all kicked it in their seventies. I've got another sister in Greely. She works at the university. Her husband is in the gas stuff up there. Rust was an only child though, so outside of my sister's bunch I guess Gus is all we got left.

Do you have any kids of your own? Deb asked.

No, said Polly, quiet for a moment. We thought we would at one point but it just never happened, so we let it go. Had pretty much settled into this life of ours till Gus come our way. We figured that was a God thing. Him comin to us. No way else for me to explain it. It's changed us.

In a good way? Green asked.

Oh the best. It's funny what you can get used to. I think life had settled into somethin like black-and-white. We were comfortable, but in retrospect, I'm not sure how happy we were. Gus has been like color comin into our lives.

Green was taken aback by how open this woman was about such personal matters. Maybe it was the boy. Most of a summer and part of a fall had passed since Gus had left the pastor's care. Tom's arrest had come in the middle of May, and a month or so after that Gus had come to live with Forest and Polly. The boy had only been in his care for four and a half months, but it felt like so much longer than that. The bond they shared that Green hoped would last a lifetime. That's what he had in common with this woman. They both knew the other had shared a form of intimacy with Gus and had that conduit between them, even if there was no immediate connection between the two.

A truck pulled up in front of the house and a man in faded jeans and work boots, binoculars hanging from a strap around his neck, got down while Gus hopped out the far side.

Come on up, Gus, said Polly. You've got visitors.

Gus climbed the steps and stood on the edge of the porch. Aloof as ever.

How you been, Gus? said Green.

Gus stared at the pastor. Squinted against the sunlight.

Don't you want to say hi, Gus? said Polly.

After a moment, Hi.

The boy hesitated. Then walked to Green and gave him a hug. The gesture brought a welling of tears to the pastor's eyes.

This is a nice place out here, said Green, half suppressing the emotion. Do you like it?

Gus shrugged.

I can tell you do, said Green. Seems like a good place to be a kid, and this Polly here is pretty nice, isn't she?

Gus didn't say anything but cracked a shy sideways smile. Turned to Polly.

Can I go see if there are any eggs?

Don't you want to visit with Mister Morris and Miss Deborah? They came all this way.

Don't worry about us, said Green. We'll be alright.

Okay then. But be sure to wash your hands after you've been in the chicken coop, like we talked about.

Yes, ma'am. And he ran off behind the house.

They sat for a while and talked. Forest sat with them. Small talk about weather and farming and life in this country. A little about Deb and Green. There wasn't much to say. Green had been the one to request this visit. They'd said it was not unheard of but definitely out of the ordinary for former foster parents to visit a child once they'd settled in a permanent home. But Gus and Polly and Forest had been open to it and so here they were. A short visit. They were there for maybe an hour. Said goodbye. Green shook Gus's hand. Accepted another hug and told him to come say hi if he was ever back in the valley. Then they drove away.

The trip down I-25 took a while. They passed through the city on the tail end of rush hour and got into Deb's sister's place late. Spent that and two more nights there. Walks beside the river and long meals, endless conversation. Green was a good fit. Deb seemed happy, which made him happy. Then it was time to go.

They drove west on Highway 50 until they came out of the flatlands and into the hill country. A sign read CAÑON CITY 20 MI, and Deb reached across and squeezed Green on the thigh.

You sure you want to do this?

Yeah. I think so. Well, I know I'll always wonder if I don't, so I guess I have to.

That's one approach, said Deb. She shook her head.

They pulled into Cañon City. Main Street stood empty of people. A few businesses amid boarded-up windows and fast-food joints. They hit the Wendy's drive-through, ate in the parking lot, and headed over to the west side of town.

You know, said Deb, I heard at one time Cañon City had a choice between hosting the Colorado University system or opening prisons. I don't know if that's true or not but it makes you think what this place might have been like if they'd gone the other way.

Lot of money in prisons, said Green.

Maybe for some. Boulder seems like it's doing a hell of a lot better than Cañon City though.

Does that mean Boulder would have gotten the prisons if Cañon City had the college?

Deb laughed. I don't know if it works like that, but maybe. Just think how different Boulder would be if they had prisons instead of a university.

Could be good for them, said Green and he smiled, though the smile faded as they pulled into a parking lot through a gate that read FEDERAL PENITENTIARY. Parked and walked in the door. Went through a security check and were led into a waiting room of sorts. Deb stayed there and Green followed a guard through another door into a room with booths, where he sat on a stool with a plate of plexiglass before him. He was there for a while before a man in an orange jumpsuit and cuffs on his wrists was led in by two guards and sat opposite him while the guards stood behind. The man's face rose, and their eyes met. He was scruffy and disheveled, but his hair and beard seemed like they got a trim from time to time. Just appeared not to give much thought to how he looked. Green thought of all the times he'd sat in a room with this man's father while doing his rounds at the Home, unaware of the connection. Almost in sync they reached for matching phone receivers and stared at each other. Listened to the other's breathing.

Well, said Tom after a time, what do you want?

Green hesitated. I guess I just wanted to see, he said.

See what.

Well, you know Gus Hawkins.

A twinkle of recognition in the man's eyes.

I know Gus Hawkins. We have that in common.

Tom took a deep breath. And that's supposed to mean what?

Doesn't mean anything. My wife was the one you duct taped to that chair that night.

She wasn't his wife, but Green thought of her as a partner and thought the word might carry more weight with this man. Why he gave any thought to what Tom Horak might think of him he couldn't say, but now that he was here he felt a drive to command some sort of respect, though he did not believe that he was accomplishing that.

You're the preacher, aint ya?

I'm a pastor. Or was. I retired.

Little young to be retirin. Or did you just realize it's all a load a crap?

Green said nothing. He wasn't going to argue with Tom, though it made him uncomfortable how close that statement came to the truth, even if he would not have put it that way.

I'm not here to discuss me or my life.

But you want to discuss mine. Seems unfair.

I'm not here to discuss your life either.

Then what in the hell do you want?

I just wanted to look you in the eyes. You've had an outsized influence on the life of a boy I love, in ways that are both terrifying and tremendously positive. I needed to see you in person. See that you exist.

Tom looked at his lap, spun the chord of the phone around a finger and let it unravel.

You must think I'm the devil, don't you.

He smiled as he said this, finding some amusement. Or wait, he said. I forgot. You don't believe in that shit anymore.

Truth is, I don't know what to think of you.

Tom snickered. You know they gave me *life* in here? No possibility of parole. I suppose that's a good thing, for society anyhow. Not so much for me. I wanted the chair, though they don't do that anymore. Lethal injection. I don't know what would be preferable. I've heard horror stories about each. I've always been afraid of needles.

Green had no response.

I heard in Utah you can request a firin squad. They're old-school out there. Mormons. They don't fuck around.

Laughed at his own joke.

Fuck it though, Tom said, batting an arm at nothing. Lettin me live was some kind of consolation prize for not killin that cop. Like I spared him or somethin. I never wanted to kill him though. Never wanted to kill no one. Just sorta happened. I aint got nothin against most people. That cop though. He's an industrious little shit. I heard he busted the door down with a fuckin sledgehammer and walked out that road in the dark.

Tom laughed so hard his eyes grew wet.

It's almost like you're enjoying yourself in there.

Tom looked around, as if just now taking in his surroundings. Held out his hands, much in the way that Green had countless times before a congregation, somber and serious, though Green doubted the sincerity of it.

It's my salvation, Tom said.

For the first time in the conversation Green wondered

what Tom's words meant to the man that spoke them. As though in response, Tom continued, You know they got me on twenty-four-hour suicide watch? I don't know why anyone cares. I guess some people think that would be an injustice for me to not spend decades in prison *thinkin bout what I done.*

He said the last part in a mocking voice.

It would save everyone a hell of a lot of money though, and I would guess there are people out there who would be happy to see me dead. Maybe you're one of em.

Green shook his head. I don't know what you deserve.

Well, I guess you're about the only one left who hasn't made up their mind.

Maybe.

They sat for a while in silence. Green had lost any sense of a plan as to how the conversation might go. There was no resolution, nothing answered. If anything, he felt more uneasy than he had before he'd sat down.

You're a God-fearin man, Tom said.

Green said nothing.

I hear this God of yours is all about forgiveness. We're all God's children? Somethin to that effect?

You could put it that way.

Well. Then. Tell me somethin.

Paused. Examined the backs of his hands, his knuckles. Green tensed, the dynamics between the two tipped off-kilter.

I aint just a murderer. Not even close. No. Not by a long
shot. I'm a human goddamn bein, just like you. I've had
things done to me. It's been a long time and there's folks
I've had to forgive, or not, but what about me?

Green waited. Tom stared.

What about you?

What about me? Where's my forgiveness? How about
a little goddamn sympathy? You got no clue what I been
through. Where's *my* salvation? He spat.

Tom was glaring. His face had gone red and a vein appeared on his forehead.

Green paused as he thought of how to respond. Recognized the contradiction Tom had made.

You think you deserve to be saved?

Why not? I'm not all that different from you, just a different set of experiences to bring me to a different outcome.

I'd never kill a man, regardless of what he'd done. It's
not in me. Not for me to judge.   ·

Oh come off it. You think you're bettern me? Hell, I
done the world a fuckin favor knockin off that son of a
bitch, and not a goddamn person in the world misses him.
Name me *one* person alive who misses that motherfucker.

Green made sure to make steady eye contact with the
man through the glass before he said, I can only think of
one.

Tom stared back, then slumped in his chair, head
bowed. All the anger drained out of him. A trickle of a tear

fell from the corner of his eye. Through the phone receiver Green heard his mumbled response.

You don't know a thing about me. Not a damn thing.

Green sat for a moment, watching the man before him. After a time he stood to leave. As he walked out through the prison halls he didn't say a word. Not to the guard who led him out or even to Deb. Walked in silence and went to the passenger seat and let Deb drive. He spent much of the remainder of the trip looking out the window. He thought about Gus and Tom. The boy's father he'd never met. Tom's father, who he had technically met, though depending on how you defined it, that was up for debate.

That night he stayed at Deb's house. He practically lived there at this point. He'd taken a job on a framing crew down valley, a skill he'd retained from younger days, and staying at her place shortened the commute. Plus he had her to come home to, and that was far from nothing.

After she had fallen asleep, she rolled on her side and put an arm across his chest, a leg up over his. The smell of her hair was in his face and it struck at something in the core of him. Through a fitful sleep he dreamed that he was looking into a pool of water. Stared at his rippled reflection that came in and out of focus and it was his face and it was Tom Horak's face and there was no discerning the two. He stared the phantom down. Looked it in the eyes and they were Tom's eyes, his eyes, the eyes of the boy, and they saw straight into his soul, saw him for the man that he was, and his own voice inside that phantom head asked the unanswerable question.

Where is my *salvation?*

He would continue to have those dreams for the rest of his life, less so over time, though he would never be free of them.

When he woke from one such dream, Deb was sleeping on her back beside him. He rested on his side. Put a hand on her stomach. She was not far enough along in her pregnancy to feel anything but he imagined that he could. He thought of his life and all he had in it compared to the years he'd spent in solitude. The people. The warmth. The family. Everything to come.

Though he did not want to wake her, he pulled Deb toward him and wrapped his arms around her, thinking to himself, *Here it is. It's this.*

This is my salvation.

Acknowledgments

First, I need to thank Amanda Birdsong. Your unconditional support for all my frivolous endeavors never ceases to boggle my mind. I love you, and I always will.

To Embry and Arlo, for bearing with me through my crash course in parenthood while I worked on bringing this book to life. You've brought joy to my life I did not know was possible.

To my family, especially my mother, who never questioned my choices and priorities, even when they made no financial sense whatsoever. Also to both of my grandmothers. To Grandma Verdella, who gave me an advance on my inheritance and told me to "write something incredible." I can't say if it's incredible or not, but I wrote. And to Grandma Pat (Crazy Gramma), who taught me to pursue my passions, even when they make no rational sense to the outside world.

Harry Kirchner's thoughtful editorial guidance has shaped this book, as well as all my writing over the last few years. Thank you for taking a chance on an unknown author. Without you, this book would not be here today.

To Dane Bahr, for everything. You're my brother and I love you.

To all my readers, through every stage of the writing process, whether you gave me feedback, kind words, or simply told me whether or not you liked it.

To Arvin Ramgoolam, for the unwavering support that you give to the literary community in our small corner of the world.

To everyone at Counterpoint and Catapult who helped make this novel a reality, and to Dan Smetanka in particular, who was open to taking a look at a second manuscript after the first one was not a good fit. Also to Wah-Ming Chang, Yukiko Tominaga, Barrett Briske, Miriam Vance, Rachel Fershleiser, Vanessa Genao, Megan Fishmann, and everyone else who was involved in this process.

Last but never least, to Jordan and Pat O'Neill. The O'Neill clan is my family. Jordan, words cannot express the gratitude I feel for all the support you've given me over the years, in every aspect of life. Until Amanda came along, you have always been my first reader and encouraged me to keep going, even when it seemed that nothing would ever come from this whole "writing thing." Thank you. Pat, you have been the best friend and mentor that one could ever have thought to ask for. You say I don't owe you a thing, and maybe that's true, but you've taught me to paint houses, run far, and dream big. Thank you for everything. You're a BAMF and I love you.

© Amanda Birdsong

C. WILLIAM LANGSFELD
lives in a small town on Colorado's
Western Slope.